Faraway Hill: Book Three

Gold Editon

This book is a work of fiction. Names, characters, places and incidents are either the products of the author's imagination or are used fictionally.

Any resemblance of any of these fictional characters to an actual person (living or deceased) is entirely coincidental.

ISBN 978-0-9963134-4-5

AUTHOR'S INTRODUCTION

Welcome to the final installment of the *Faraway Hill* saga. As you can probably imagine, writing this trilogy has been like writing a complicated, 40-chapter novel. While I did have a general idea of where the story would go, I also allowed my characters to provide some direction as well. This meant I had the added challenge of keeping straight various plot points and developments.

The key tools for me were synopses. After finishing each chapter, I wrote a condensed version of the action. This allowed me a resource to avoid any major contradictions.

Soap operas are regularly derided as silly, melodramatic entertainment. They are often guilty of this, and the trilogy was written with that in mind (could there be any convention that's soapier than Greg's coma and subsequent partial amnesia?). However, I have since developed a considerable respect for the writers of daytime dramas. It's a challenge to keep stories and characters fresh, interesting and still be welcome into a viewer's home. It's also a challenge to stay true to your show's history --- a history that long-term fans know quite well. This is why soaps have not one writer but whole staffs led by a head writer and a producer all guided by a "bible" that keeps track of who is who and who did what.

In any event, I hope that you've enjoyed my silly, melodramatic entertainment. The saga wraps up in such a way that leaves the door open for future installments should readers show enough interest and should I come up with more stories.

Until then, thanks again for reading *Faraway Hill*.

James A. Richards, author
Faraway Hill

EPISODE ONE

Some moments are better than others. Some moments should be savored, relished, thoroughly enjoyed. There are so few of these moments in life.

Karen St. John is having just such a moment. Regal in her designer gown and exuding movie star charisma, the stunning middle aged woman is guest of honor at the Currier Museum of Art. New Hampshire's most important citizens are here: the state's governor; US Senator Richard Davis and his child bride Ann Halloran; business leaders; philanthropists; reporters. Even the famous artist Agnes Gabler --- in her 90s, sitting proud in a wheelchair --- is gracing the event. All of these people are smiling. All of them are applauding. They are applauding only one person. They are applauding Karen.

Karen begins her speech, about her donation that made the museum's latest acquisition possible. But in the back of her mind are different thoughts about this moment; something that is making this moment even more precious to her. For as she talks about Willem Arondeus --- the artist whose illustrations are being added to the museum's collection --- three people who have hurt her or her little girl are being dealt with. All of them are being removed with the help of Daddy's logic. Karen could tell that everything was working as planned when two guests rushed out of the museum. That means this moment is not just better than other moments. This moment is a nearly perfect moment. Karen is sure of that. There is no question in her mind.

That is, until <u>he</u> enters the room.

****

By rights it should only take a few minutes to get from the museum to the shop. All Julie Halloran has to do is drive down Ash Street, turn right onto Bridge Street and that takes her directly to Elm. But the moment they pass the Chestnut Street intersection --- only a few blocks from Elm Street --- they are stopped. Police are out directing people north and away from the scene. *Holy shit, is it really that bad?*

Julie rolls down the window to call one of the officers over. "We think the fire is at our store. Is there anyway we can get there or talk to someone?"

The officer, a woman, steps away and pulls out her walkie talkie to speak to what Julie suspects is her superior. She turns to her mother, Eve King, who is sitting in the car's passenger seat just finishing a call on her cell. "Mary says that all of the employees are safe."

"Thank God for that." Mary is the young college girl who has become Julie's right hand in running their little book, gift and coffee shop in the heart of downtown Manchester.

The officer returns to the car. "Ma'am, if you park over there on Church Street, another officer will meet you. You'll have to walk, but he'll take you to the fire marshal." Julie thanks her and follows her instructions. Within a moment, another officer, a handsome young man, greets them. "Are you ladies the owners of King's Korner?"

"Yes, I'm Julie Halloran; this is my mother, Eve King."

"I'm Lieutenant Aaron Tracey. Please follow me." He leads them down Nutfield Lane --- a little street one block east of Elm --- until they reach Amherst and walk up to Manchester's main drag. A huge section of Elm is blocked off with fire trucks, ambulance and police cars. WMUR-TV has a mobile van on the scene. People crowd the sidewalks to watch the firefighters at work. *Oh my God,* Julie thinks. *It looks like an entire block was hit.* She glances at her mother, who appears calm and controlled even though their little business is now a black char.

Lt. Tracey advises them to wait here, until he can get someone to answer their questions. Julie takes her mother's hand in hers, and gives it a supportive squeeze. The crowds seem to be getting bigger when she sees a familiar face. *Is that Mark Bradley? What the hell is he doing here?* A year ago he was just a farm hand who married her best friend. Then everyone was stunned to learn that he was earning extra money as a male escort. He soon disappeared. Julie thought the man was out of their lives forever.

The fire chief walks over and introduces himself. "Mrs. King, Mrs. Halloran, I'm sorry to say that it's totaled."

"Any idea what caused it?"

"We won't know until the investigation is complete, but we think it may be electrical."

That makes no sense, Julie thinks; *we had the place rewired before opening the shop.* Another fireman motions the chief who excuses himself.

"Don't worry mom, we're insured."

"I know, but . . . it still hurts."

The chief returns, this time with a grim look on his face. Something else is wrong, very wrong. "Ladies, I'm sorry again, but . . . we found a body inside."

"Oh my God! Any idea who it is?"

"We found his ID." With a great deal of genuine sympathy he looks directly at Julie's mother and says, "It's your husband, ma'am; it's Senator King."

****

It took some effort, but Little Jack is finally down for the night. Jack Campbell is surprised at how tenacious his son can be. He came up with all sorts of excuses to stay up as long as possible. Jack has had to negotiate plenty of business deals in his life --- not too mention sweet talk many people into bed --- but reasoning with a clever six-year-old is more challenging than he thought.

Jack returns to the living room where his husband, Joe Westbrook, is sitting on the sofa watching an old movie on TV. "Did he finally give up?" Joe asks with a sly smile.

"Yeah, I finally had to read *Where The Wild Things Are* again."

Joe winces a little. He needs to take another pain pill. Without saying a word, Jack steps into their bedroom, picks up the bottle and brings it to him. Joe thanks him with a smile and takes a pill with a swallow of Diet Coke. Jack sits next to him, trying to not look as worried as he feels. But he knows their days together are numbered: his husband, a transsexual who used to Jack's girlfriend, is dying of ovarian cancer.

The image on the screen abruptly changes to a Channel 9 news graphic. An attractive woman with short blonde hair and an intense gaze appears in the studio. "Good evening, this is Tiffany Eddy in the WMUR newsroom with a breaking story . . ."

****

" . . . A fire has snarled much of downtown Manchester as a popular shop is destroyed. Firefighters also report the discovery of a body inside. We go to Sean McDonald live on the scene."

Sitting in their living room, Lorene Gale and her fiancée Vivian Bickel are watching the same news report. The two women, both in their 40s, one white and the other black, have been enjoying a quiet evening together. After years and thousands of miles apart, they are now sharing Lorene's farm and home and loving every minute of it.

"Thank you Tiffany," the handsome young man says. Behind him they can see fire trucks and police cars and crowds. "Elm Street is just now opening up to traffic as officials begin their investigation of a fire at King's Korner, a book and coffee shop owned by the wife and daughter of United States Senator Benjamin King. I spoke to the fire marshal just before going on the air who tells me that a body has been found inside and that it has been tentatively identified, although they are not releasing the victim's name just yet . . ."

****

The ride back to Concord is quiet; too quiet, as far as Ann Halloran Davis is concerned. Her husband hasn't said much since last night. It worries her.

Right now they are tooling up 93 after Richard did some clever navigating through Manchester's chaos. Much of the city traffic is being detoured because of the fire. It saddens her to know that Ben is gone. She left a couple of voicemails for Julie, but hasn't heard back yet. Ann remembers growing up how jealous she was of her best friend, for the father she had. Ben was handsome and respected; a successful lawyer with his office in one of Manchester's finest buildings. He and his wife Eve had renovated an old colonial house in Faraway Hill into something close to a showcase. Ben was very different from Munroe Gale, the man Ann thought was her father. Munroe never seemed to succeed at anything. Whenever faced with a failure --- and there were many --- he hid in the safety of a bottle. But in the end even vodka couldn't protect Munroe, who took another man's life before taking his own.

Ann reaches out to her husband and gives his upper arm a gentle but supportive squeeze. Richard Davis is the state's senior US Senator and now, once again, the state's only senator. With Ben King's death, New Hampshire has lost two senators in six months.

It still amazes her that someone so remarkable, so accomplished as Richard Davis would be interested in her. Ann is in her early 20s, still very much the young farm girl trying to be more than she is. Richard is in his mid 50s, hair graying and a handsome face creased with years of life experience. Moreover, she is Lewis Halloran's bastard daughter and the subject of so much gossip and scandal. Yesterday was another scandal averted. Her first husband, a male prostitute named Mark Bradley, had been blackmailing them. Mark had cleverly made her think their divorce last year was valid; it wasn't. Richard paid him off after having him sign the necessary papers. When they first learned of the fraud, Richard was strong and stoic, insisting that "you are Mrs. Davis now" and would solve the problem. But ever since confronting Mark he has said very little.

That silence is louder than any scream.

****

It has never been easy for Karen to keep her anger at bay. But the sight of a smiling Greg Halloran walking into the museum's elegant Winter Garden at her perfect moment nearly made her scream.

She had a carefully crafted and executed plan. Karen had hired a gentleman from Boston, a professional who knows how to create an "accident". She then cleverly arranged to have three men --- Mark Bradley, Greg Halloran and Ben King --- gather at Eve's little shop where they were supposed to meet their end. A grieving Julie, having lost both father and husband, would turn to her beloved Aunt Karen who would reveal the truth: that Aunt Karen is really her mother. Together with Julie's baby son, they would live happily ever after as a family in the big famous Halloran mansion.

The plan had the added benefit of ridding herself of Mark Bradley --- the hustler who used to service her as a client and then foolishly chose to blackmail her --- and of hurting her sister, Eve; the woman who stole Karen's little girl.

It should have worked. But seeing Greg meant that something went wrong, very wrong. News of the fire arrived soon after causing the gala to end early. Details were unavailable, but if Greg survived it is entirely possible that Mark did, too. Only Ben has been lost. That isn't good enough.

Like so many people, she had to drive around the closed off section of Manchester to get to the highway. Somehow Karen managed to stay calm going back to Faraway Hill.

That calm evaporates the moment she's home.

Karen slams the door shut and lets out the primal, angry cry she has been holding in for half an hour. Without thought to anything, she starts grabbing objects, throwing vases and lamps against a wall or to the floor. Pulling down the painting of Lake Winnipesauke from above her fireplace; shredding upholstery with a ceramic shard. All the while, the most vile words and thoughts and images crowd her mind.

Finally, exhausted, Karen slips to the floor, sobbing amid the ruins of her once beautiful living room.

✶✶✶✶

Greg Halloran must take the long way home. He has no choice. Parts of Elm were still tied up from the fire when he and Agnes Gabler left the Currier Museum together.

"I'm very worried about Eve," Agnes says softly. She is sitting in the car next to him, her wheelchair folded up in the backseat. Greg nods gently in her direction, noticing the lines on the elderly woman's face and realizes that artist must have seen plenty of tragedy in her 95 years.

He's worried about Eve, too, and about Julie. But he is also worried that someone will find out he was at the shop shortly before the fire. That bastard Mark Bradley had suggested they meet at King's Korner to settle up his blackmail. He was looking forward to getting rid of the dude. Last year, Mark was working secretly as a male prostitute while living in Faraway Hill --- and taped them fucking. Ever since, Greg's has been covering the rent on Bradley's expensive New York apartment to keep him from posting the video online.

Greg expected the meeting at the closed store to be swift. What he didn't expect was his father-in-law. Bradley had a good laugh angering and embarrassing him and Ben King: letting Greg know that Mark is the senator's illegitimate son --- a surprise that shocked him --- and Ben know that Greg was his "favorite client". Mark left after both men paid him off. Then the two of them had it out about Greg cheating on Ben's daughter. Greg knew he couldn't defend himself and didn't even try. Ben insisted on being left alone to cool down. "We'll discuss this later," his father-in-law told him sternly. Greg went by himself to the Currier. *The fire must have started just after I left.*

It only takes a few minutes to arrive at Faraway Hill. The town is just north of Manchester. The summer sun is slowly setting, gracing the charming little buildings with a warm glow. Faraway Hill used to be one of New Hampshire's many textile towns. But today only the Halloran mill remains. Instead, Faraway Hill is a tourist center. Even tonight, as they drive through town, Greg and Agnes can see visitors casually strolling through the square, gazing up at the statute of its founder --- and Greg's ancestor --- John Halloran.

They arrive at the Halloran mansion, a stately Georgian home built two centuries ago and modeled after the original White House. Greg pulls up under the portico where a maid greets them. Together they help Agnes into her wheelchair and enter through the beautiful Grant Vestibule. Once inside, Frederick, the family's aging butler informs them that "Mrs. Halloran has insisted her mother spend the evening. She feels it would be best if Mrs. King weren't alone tonight."

Greg nods in agreement. "Where are they?"

"Upstairs, sir."

Agnes urges him to go up right away without her. "I'm still peckish; the party ended before anyone could eat." Frederick wheels her off to the kitchen while Greg climbs the marble Grand Staircase. He finds Eve in the nursery, holding her grandson, her eyes puffy and red from crying. Greg kisses her cheek like a good son-in-law and tells her how sorry he is.

"Thank you."

"Any idea what happened?"

"Right now they think it was something electrical."

Greg isn't sure what more to say but can't help but wonder: *does she know about Ben and Mark? What else does she know?* Eve smiles at baby Johnny, "I love holding him."

"Me too; it's almost . . . therapeutic."

"It's like I can feel his unconditional love."

"Where's Julie?"

"In your suite."

Greg crosses the hall and enters the master suite's large oval parlor. His wife is pacing beside the settee, cell phone in use, handling things like an efficient manager. Still, he can see she's been crying.

"Thank you, Victoria, I appreciate everything. Just email me the draft and I'll get back to you right away." She looks up with a smile, happy to see her husband despite all of the problems they've been having. Their wedding night was ruined by the murder of Greg's father, Lewis Halloran, who was shot to death by a disturbed farmer named Munroe Gale. The farmer took his own life soon after, but their nightmare didn't end with him. Everyone soon learned that Julie's best friend, Munroe's daughter Ann, is really Lewis' child. Dealing with that revelation gave the couple nothing but grief for months. Eventually, Greg reunited with Jack Campbell, his college lover. Julie found out the truth shortly after the birth of their son. They've been sleeping in separate rooms since. Only since Greg's recent heath scare --- a coma --- have they reached some sort of détente.

"That was Dad's chief of staff. She's working on a press release. They also expect reporters showing up tomorrow, so I have to call Peter Brandt and make sure there are some officers outside to handle them."

Greg looks at her, and sees the beautiful and strong young woman he fell in love with. Even now, eyes red and face carved in sadness, she takes his breath away. Greg doesn't say anything. He doesn't have to. He simply walks up to Julie and wraps his arms around his wife. She begins to sob, tears drenching his shoulder.

****

It's the last thing she expected to see, and it scares her.

Denise Sullivan is a party girl from way back. She has woken up in plenty of trashed dorm rooms and apartments, often with a headache and wondering where she is. But this morning is different. When Denise arrives as her boss' home, the sight is shocking: Karen St. John's living room has been totaled. Every pricey vase and lamp has been smashed. The designer sofa and chairs have had their upholstery shredded. Even the wonderful painting of Lake Winnipesauke that hung over the fireplace has been snapped in two and lying on the floor. It's as if some wild animal was set loose.

Or that someone broke in. *Oh, my God . . .*

Panicked, she calls out "Mrs. St. John! Are you here? Are you alright?"

"Of course, dear," comes a calm sweet voice. Denise enters the dining room to find her boss, as elegant as always; eating her croissant and reading this morning's *Union Leader* about Senator King's death. "Why wouldn't I be?"

Seeing her like this, as if nothing had happened, is somehow far more frightening than the living room. "They've written such a nice story about Ben," Mrs. St. John comments sweetly. "I'm sure poor Eve appreciates it."

"The living room --- "

"Oh, yes, be sure to have someone clean it up. Then have that fey little man from Boston in to redo it."

"Yes, but . . . what happened?"

Mrs. St. John looks up from her paper, a serene smile on her face, and explains simply "I just feel its time for a change."

****

The room's décor isn't quite right. This is true of the entire suite. The white furniture is faux French provincial, something common in many young girls' bedrooms. But the walls and carpet don't match. They really don't belong here. Several months ago, Julie Halloran had everything hastily moved here from the suite across the hall. That suite and its furnishings belonged to Greg's Aunt Joan as she grew up in the mansion. She always stayed there when visiting. But when Ann decided to move in, she was assigned the other suite to keep her as far away from everyone else as possible. This was the compromise and no one was happy about it.

No one is happy this morning, either. Already reporters are showing up outside. The Faraway Hill Unified Police Force has officers keeping them at bay. Every news agency across the country is headlining the latest death of a New Hampshire senator. To everyone else, Ben King was a lawyer or a politician. But to Eve, he was a lover and a husband and a father. He was everything.

Sitting in this mismatched room, on a chair meant for someone much younger, Eve looks out her window onto the mansion's beautiful garden. This, she knows, is why Julie gave her these rooms. The suite across the hall, the one Joan and then Ann called home, looks out on the front lawn where the camera crews are sitting and watching. Here she can see the blooming of flowers and trees, the view of life.

A gentle rap on the door; "come in." Julie enters a warm and loving smile on her face. "Good morning, Mom; how are you feeling?"

"I'm fine."

"We were hoping you'd have breakfast with us."

"I know," Eve gestures at a tray of half-eaten eggs and bacon. "I'm just not up for much company right now."

Julie gently closes the door and sits in the pink chair next to her mother's pink chair. "Agnes wants to come in later today." The artist has been staying at the Halloran mansion while her own home, a famous former sugar house, is renovated.

"I'd like that."

"Are you . . . up to talking about the arrangements, yet?"

Eve smiles proudly. She has always admired her little girl's ability to handle any situation. It is a natural strength Eve saw in her father. It reminds her of what a blessing Ben was; he set aside his own pride to raise Eve's niece as their own child. Never in 25 years of marriage did he ever utter a word of doubt or regret.

"Of course."

"By the way, Aunt Karen called earlier. Just to check on everyone. I told her we were doing okay."

Eve nods, but can't help think of how many problems her baby sister has caused and could still create now that Eve is all alone, without Ben's strength to buoy her. "I don't want to talk about Karen. Let's talk about how we'll say goodbye to your father."

✳✳✳✳

Greg Halloran steps into his father's study --- which is <u>his</u> study now --- and plops into the big leather chair behind the desk. Breakfast was a quiet affair this morning. No one said very much. Eve stayed upstairs. It was sad to see the reporters gather outside, not to mention the headline in today's *Union Leader*.

Still sitting on the desk is the file folder he found yesterday. On it is written in his father's hand, "Greg & the Brothers". He opens it to find lined yellow sheets with comments by Lewis such as "ask about initiation process for older plebes" and "get Robert to help lobby the elders." He keeps seeing references to "The Brothers" and "Brothers of Thebes." None of this makes any sense to him, so Greg does what anyone in the 21st century does: he boots up his father's computer. It's been awhile, so Windows immediately begins to update the antivirus software. Once that is done, he launches Explorer and Googles "Brothers of Thebes".

There isn't much here. Typically a Google search yields thousands of results. But there appear to be only a couple of dozen. Most of the listings are blogs filled with weird comments from weird bloggers who are convinced someone (or some thing) is secretly ruling the world. But what catches Greg's eye is a link to Wikipedia. He clicks it and the following entry appears:

> **The Brothers of Thebes** (thĕbz), is an alleged secret society of influential men that traces its history to the early days of the United States.
>
> Many historians contend that the Brothers are strictly a legend and has never existed while several conspiracy theorists insist that the society is not only real but very active behind the scenes of American politics and economy.
>
> ### Origins of Name
> The society's name was inspired by the Sacred Band of Thebes, a troop of elite citizen soldiers consisting of 150 to 300 male couples drawn from the ancient Greek city of Thebes.
>
> According to the historian and essayist Plutarch, the band was organized by the Theban commander Gorgidas in 378 BCE who encouraged the men to be sexually intimate as a means of cementing their loyalty to the corps.

The band was considered extremely successful. Their peak came in 375 BCE when the band routed a Spartan army three times its size during a battle at the ancient Greek city of Tegra. The corps' defeat finally came in 338 BCE at the Battle of Chaerpnea. Despite their strength, the troops were no match for the innovative long-speared Macedonian phalanx.

Around 300 BCE, the citizens of Thebes erected a memorial on the band's burial site of a giant stone lion. This memorial was restored in the 20th century and still stands today.

Origins of the Brothers of Thebes

Legend has it that the Brothers were formed in the late 1700s by a group of American men who were either not interested in or not welcome in more established societies such as the Freemasons. Most of these men were "gatekeepers", those who worked as secretaries and aides-de-camp for many of the new country's leaders. As such they regularly had access to confidential information that was used to benefit themselves and other members.

Eventually some of the Founding Fathers, many of them Freemasons, also allegedly joined the Brothers.

The Brothers Lodge

The Brothers are supposedly based in a secret lodge located somewhere in New England, although it has never been located and its existence is disputed.

Descriptions of the lodge vary depending on the story. One story calls it a vast, underground structure. Another story describes it as a large stone, Gothic building. At least one tale claims that the lodge is a virtual place, not a real one, and exists wherever the Brothers' elders meet.

Membership & Governance

Membership is largely a matter of legacy; that is only the sons, grandsons and nephews of existing or past Brothers are allowed to apply for consideration.

It remains unclear how the society is ruled, but it is believed to be by a council of elders who have achieved a certain amount of respect and longevity.

The Ritual Use of Latin

Legend has it that the Brothers use Latin phrases to greet and acknowledge each other as well as in formal rituals.

Skeptics point out that this is another reason the Brothers must be a myth, explaining that an organization inspired by an ancient Theban army would use Greek rather than Latin for such purposes.

The Brothers Initiation Process

It is believed that the initiation process is an extensive program of classes, physical training and sexual activities. All inspired by the Sacred Band of Thebes.

Details are murky but most legends describe the process as placing a heavy emphasis on sexual experiences between the plebes and between a plebe and his tutor. The goal is similar to that of the Sacred Band of Thebes: to bind the Brothers together in the most intimate manner possible. Whether the members consider themselves straight, bisexual or gay remains a matter of controversy among conspiracy theorists who often fixate their stories on the process.

The Alleged Powers

There are different theories as to how powerful the Brothers of Thebes actually is. Some believe that they control national elections and the stock market. Others believe that they are extremely influential but don't actually control anything. A common belief is that the Brothers act as a sort of high-class mob, functioning to benefit its members and able to take out its enemies.

Whatever their capabilities, nearly all theorists agree that the Brothers greatest strength is its ability to exist and function discreetly.

Doubts about the Brothers

Most historians and scholars consider the Brothers of Thebes to be strictly a myth, pointing out that it would be nearly impossible to keep the existence of the society secret for so long.

In 1974 a man named Thomas Walters, part of a storied
Vermont timber family, self-published a book called *Inside
the Brothers*. In it, Walters supposedly describes the
initiation process in detail. He also claimed in interviews that
all the copies were destroyed in a warehouse fire ordered by
the elders. Walters died in a hunting accident in 1978.

In 1989, an article in *Vanity Fair* by Gore Vidal called tales
of the Brothers of Thebes to be strictly a myth that originated
in Colonial America. Vidal's essay claimed that the legend
was begun by British Loyalists trying to de-legitimize the
new country. Conspiracy theorists charged Vidal with trying
to cover up the Brothers' existence at the society's request.

In 1992, Warner Brothers considered doing a film inspired
by the Brothers of Thebes legend, but development stopped
six months later. No reason was given.

This is very strange, why would Dad be so interested in this ridiculous legend?
Before he can investigate further, Greg's cell rings; it's Jack Campbell, who asks
him "Hey dude, how is everyone holding up?"

"As well as can be expected, I guess."

"Are you going into the office today?"

"No, but Patrick will be there." Greg's cousin, Patrick Halloran, has been helping
out recently. The poor kid is dividing his time between Yale, visiting his
institutionalized mother and working with him at the family business. The load
has been heavy on the young man. But he'll be graduating soon and that should
make things easier for him.

"So, what's the plan?"

"Julie thinks she'll need to go to her parents' home and get papers --- you know,
will and life insurance and all. I think I should go with her."

Jack is quiet a moment, a very brief moment, before answering "of course, she
needs you now."

"Are <u>you</u> okay?"

"Yeah . . . just missing you." The two men have had trouble connecting for a long time. Greg knows that most of this is his fault. He is in love with two people and just can't seem to make a choice.

"Remember Greg, no matter what: I love you."

****

It seems as if the Boston's beloved Union Oyster House is always busy, with people filling booths and tables to enjoy the restaurant's famous seafood. When she was a young woman struggling to succeed, Karen Scott would sit at the famous circular oyster bar savoring whatever she could afford, just for the sake of being here. But today, she has driven out here for a purpose, a very special purpose. Karen St. John is angry. And only one man can explain what went wrong.

The hostess seats her not far from the famous Kennedy Booth, so named in honor of the president who was among the restaurant's many famous patrons. Her own booth isn't all that different: the seats' high backs cut off much of the noise, creating a little cocoon of privacy.

Karen has barely looked at her menu when the man arrives. He slides into the seat across from her. The man doesn't bother to greet her. He simply says, "I figured that I'd hear from you."

"It didn't work."

"That's not my fault."

"Then who's is it?"

"Come on, lady, you know as well as anyone there is things we can't control. The guy --- the hooker --- he changed the meeting time at the last minute. I couldn't do anything about that. You couldn't do anything about that."

He's probably right, she thinks, *Daddy always warned that logic fails when people fail to act logically or predictably.* Still, she was hoping for more of an explanation. "Well, then, I'll just have to come up with something else."

****

Having failed repeatedly to get Julie or Mrs. King on the phone, Ann Davis decides to simply drive in to Faraway Hill. But arriving turns out to be anything but simple: the Halloran mansion has been cordoned off by the local police while reporters and camera crews wait outside. She can see one cable news reporter doing his stand-up with the great house framed behind him.

Fortunately an officer recognizes her. *There are benefits to being a hometown girl*, she thinks, *even a notorious one.* The officer smiles and guides her car past the check point so that she can pull up to the portico where another familiar face greets her. This is her old friend Peter Brandt, looking handsome in his uniform. Peter and Ann used to date in high school. In those days he was just a nice kid without any serious direction in his life. But today is chief of the Faraway Hill Unified Police Department, overseeing three neighboring towns. And he's still in his twenties. *Go figure.*

"Hi, Ann."

"Hi, Peter. Those reporters are nuts."

"Tell me about it. We had to corral them just a little while ago so that Julie could leave."

Damn, I wanted to see her. "She left? Where to?"

Peter looks up to see the reporters, not far away, paying them a little too much attention. "Maybe we should take a little walk."

Ann follows him to the rear of the house, where the famous Halloran garden is blooming. The cavalcade of colors is stunning. She saw little of this when she lived here, having moved in during fall. But now she is enveloped by a little bit of Eden.

Mark gently takes her hand in his. It reminds her of the old days, when they used to walk like this through Faraway Hill's main square. "Julie and Greg went to her mother's house to get some papers."

"How is Mrs. King? I know that she's been staying here."

"I haven't seen her myself, but I'm sure she's having a tough time."

"I'm sure she is." Ann stops to admire some of the roses. There are so many flowers here, including some she can't identify. Still, there is a beauty and serenity to their surroundings.

"You seem to be having a tough time, too."

"What makes you say that?"

"The look on your face --- and the fact that your ex has been seen around town."

Fuck. That mean Mark was making sure people see him, just to humiliate her. "What are people saying about me now?"

"Not much; mostly it's been about him. Any idea why he's back?"

Ann shrugs.

"Come on, Ann, you can tell me."

"Well . . . promise me you won't tell anyone. Not even Julie knows."

"Okay."

"Mark showed up on my wedding day."

"He did? I never saw him."

"Oh, found a way to sneak up to my suite. He had a wedding present for me."

"What?"

"That he was still my husband."

"Come again?"

"He faked the divorce. It's true; Richard checked. When Mark heard I was marrying again he knew this was his opportunity to make some quick cash. Richard just paid him off the other day."

"That fucker."

"Well, hopefully he'll be gone soon. But Richard has been acting very strangely ever since. He worries me, Peter; he really does."

"How so?"

"I think that he's come to realize what a mistake he made --- what a mistake I am."

****

Denise lucked out and met a young girl in town named Meryl who agreed, no questions asked and at the right price, to clean up the devastation in Mrs. St. John's living room. "I just need the money," she said.

The girl has done a good job; the broken pieces are gone. All that remains are the shredded furniture. A junk dealer will pick those up tomorrow. But one thing that can't be easily cleared away is the fear that keeps gnawing at her. Denise is beginning to understand that her glamorous, amazing boss is hiding a dark side; a terrible dark side. And she needs to protect herself.

"Or," she mutters out loud to no one in particular, "maybe I should just get the fuck out of here."

It suddenly occurs to Denise that maybe, just maybe, there is more she needs to know. She climbs the stairs up to Mrs. St. John's immaculate bedroom. Denise examines each painting and piece of furniture, thinking *where would she put it?*

On a hunch, she opens the closet and there it is: sitting on the shelf, next to a file box. This is the "special package" that Mrs. St. John ordered from her New York attorney just a few days ago. It has already been opened. Denise reaches in and pulls out the documents inside. One look and there is only one thing she can say.

"Holy shit!"

****

If feels strange being here, is the first thing Julie thinks as she opens the door. This house is where she spent most of her life. She remembers being a child here, with different rooms closed at different times while her parents struggled to pay for the renovations. There were weeks on end when something would be under construction. When rooms were being painted, all of the furniture would be covered by sheets and tarps. When the plumbing was being replaced, they stayed in a motel nearby. And when a blizzard collapsed part of the roof, it began to snow in her bedroom. To her parents, these were frustrating problems. But to their little girl, it meant every day was an adventure.

Even now, as Julie wanders through the finished living room, she can remember holidays by candlelight and birthday parties with lopsided cake (her mother was always a terrible baker).

"Are you okay?" Greg gently asks her. He insisted on coming along. Julie is glad he did. They've been getting along so well lately that she has been appreciating another memory: of why she fell in love with him, why she married him. "Yeah, I guess so. You know, the Christmas Tree always goes in that corner. Dad always wanted to have a real tree, but Mom hated the fuss of taking care of one. So he bought this really expensive one when I was, oh, I don't know, maybe twelve, and he assembled it in the same place just after Thanksgiving."

Greg steps behind her and places his warm, loving arms around her. It feels good, being embraced by him, just like when they were dating. It's hard to imagine that was just a year ago; so much has happened since it often feels like a decade has past.

After a moment, they walk into Ben's study. It is smaller and less ornate than the one in the Halloran mansion. But to Julie, it's just as special and just as dignified. There is a handsome fireplace with built-in, matching bookshelves and a heavy old desk her mother found at a flea market. "I think they keep everything in this drawer."

Greg opens part of the desk and finds a collection of manila file folders. They are all marked different subjects, like the tax year. One is labeled "will" and another "life insurance". But as he pulls these out, another one gets his attention. This folder is marked "Julie's papers." Greg hands it to her, "any idea what that's about?"

"Nope, never saw it before," she says opening it. One look at the documents inside and all she can say is, "holy shit!"

EPISODE TWO

Greg's wife rarely swears. It just isn't her style. So hearing Julie cry "holy shit," he knows something is wrong; very wrong. The look on her face is just as troubling. It's as if she's just been slapped in the face. *What could it be?* She hands him the papers. They are the last thing he would ever expect to find.

One is a birth certificate. Issued in Hillsborough County, it lists the father as unknown, the mother as Karen Scott --- and the child as Julie Scott. The others are all relating to an adoption of the child Julie by Ben and Eve King. *Holy shit is right.* "Julie, this means ---"

"That Aunt Karen is my mother."

****

Jack is trying to assess what to keep. Ever since his hurried wedding, he's been spending most of his time upstairs in Joe's apartment with their son.

Last December they moved into separate apartments in the same complex. Located on Pennacook Street, it is one of a group of buildings constructed in the early 1900s by a developer named Edwin L. Gresley. The exterior features towering Corinthian columns and elegant balconies; the interiors have wood trim, built-in cabinets and stain glass windows.

Soon they will be moving again. Joe wants to buy a house before he is gone. Planning for the man's death is something Jack is having a hard time with. So far their little boy knows nothing except that his papa is sick. They haven't figured out how to tell him.

Jack's cell rings. It's Denise Sullivan. He frowns at seeing her name on the screen. Back in college, he and Denise hooked up often. Greg Halloran also fucked her several times. Neither man ever expected to see her after graduation, but she showed up last year as Karen St. John's new assistant. He's ended up with her again a few times since. "Hey Denise, what's up?"

"I need to see you," she answers urgently. "Right away, today." Her voice sounds panicky.

"What's wrong?"

"I can't tell you now, but it's big; really big. I have to come into Manchester, is there any place we can meet? Any place private?"

"Look, Denise, don't take this the wrong way, but if you want to hook-up ---."

"Shit, that's not it. I found out something, something that could hurt Greg and his wife. Meet with me. Pick a place."

Jack suggests a pub in Manchester and they set a time this afternoon. *What the fuck could it be?* She won't say more on the phone, so he'll have to wait.

****

Greg is waiting and watching his wife, who is sits there, reading and rereading the documents.

"I just don't get it," she mumbles repeatedly.

They've returned to the living room and are next to each other on the sofa. Greg has no idea what to expect from her. *Will she cry? Will she scream?* He can't even imagine how he would react. Eventually, she looks up at him, a tear streaming down her cheek. "It must be true," she says softly.

"I'm sorry."

"Greg, I don't know what to do now, what to think. Hell, I don't even know how to face either of them. Should I confront Mom, Karen, what?"

"You're asking me?"

The irony makes her smile. Greg had his own complicated parental relationships. Not to mention the odd triangle the two of them are part of. "I guess so."

"Don't say anything."

"But ---."

"Hear me out: Eve has just lost her husband. Would it really be right for her to lose her daughter, too?"

"I can't avoid it Greg, I can't avoid them."

"Maybe, but you need time to think and digest. And your mom has too much to deal with right now."

She nods in agreement. "You know what's interesting?"

"More interesting than this?"

"Please don't make me laugh," Julie smiles through her damp cheeks. "When I was pregnant, I kept turning to Mom for advice. You know, morning sickness, backache, all of it. She couldn't offer any. But Aunt Karen had all sorts of tips. I remember thinking at the time how weird that was. I guess we know why. And there's something else."

"What?"

"You, Ann and I: our birthdays are just weeks apart. We already know that Lewis got Lorene pregnant shortly after your mother. And Lorene worked in the mansion with Karen."

"So it's possible she knows something. Maybe that's what you should do first; talk to Lorene."

****

Lorene looks up at the bright, clear sky and smiles. Despite the tragic news about Senator King, she feels like her life has never been better. She and her fiancée, Vivian, have just left Dave's Diner, a popular eatery a block from Faraway Hill's main square. The owner and his wife --- like almost everyone in town --- have been wonderfully supportive of the couple. "I've never seen you so happy," Dave remarks.

Holding hands, the two ladies do a little window shopping. Vivian notices a chair in the consignment shop's window, and they discuss the interesting new pieces at Sandburg's Jewelers. But their pleasant afternoon changes abruptly when the handsome young man steps up to them.

"Hey there, Lorene; your looking good."

Mark Bradley stands before the couple with his cocky smile. Lorene heard that her former son-in-law has been sighted around town. "Hello Mark, why are you in Faraway Hill?"

"Just checking up things. I guess your Vivian, huh?"

"Yes, young man," Vivian says eying him cautiously. "I take it you are Annie's ex-husband."

Mark bows before them like a mocking court jester. "And I've heard you've embraced the lezbo lifestyle. I guess that's all the rage these days."

"Don't be so crass; I haven't forgotten how you hurt and humiliated my daughter."

"Wow, Lor; you've grown some serious balls since we last met. I guess that makes you the bottom, Viv."

"Leave town."

"No can do, Mamma Gale. I have one last piece of business." Bare headed, he tips an imaginary hat to the ladies and strolls on. Vivian watches him carefully until he rounds the corner and out of sight. "I wonder what he means by that."

****

This is Jack's second visit to Shaskeen Pub, a popular Manchester spot just across from City Hall Plaza. He walked in for the first time just the other day, and was impressed with the comfortable surroundings and especially the handsome bar. The bartender had told him that the wood came from a church in Ireland and was custom built for the place.

That afternoon he was meeting Greg Halloran, hoping that after everything the two men have been through the past couple of years, they can finally plan a life together. But Jack saw how torn his lover truly is, between him and his wife. When they parted, Greg assured him by saying "you won't be alone". But with Julie's dad dying, Jack is becoming less and less sure. Joe will be gone in a few months. *If Greg stays with his wife, what the hell will I do?*

"Hey."

Jack looks up to see Denise Sullivan, poured into a tight blouse and jeans. She has always liked to show off her body. She was known for strutting around NYU, swinging her well-formed ass for everyone to see and enjoy. But today Denise isn't here to seduce. Jack can actually see fear on her face. After they order a couple of drinks, she pulls some papers from her purse. "You need to see these. They're photocopies I made this morning."

He unfolds them to find the copy of a birth certificate and some other documents. The information is stunning. "Holy shit! Where did you get these?"

"Mrs. St. John. They were in a 'special package' she ordered from her New York attorney."

"She gave them to you?"

"No, Jack, she doesn't know I found them. And there's more. Yesterday morning I arrived at her house --- and the living room, the entire living room, had been trashed."

"Trashed? There was a robbery?"

"No, I think Mrs. St. John did it. I think she did it all by herself."

"I don't get it."

"Upholstery was ripped; vases and lamps shattered. She had this wonderful painting over the fireplace. But when I got there it was broken in two on the floor. It's as if she went wild or something."

"Shit, what did she say about it?"

"That's the weirdest part of all; I found her eating breakfast as if nothing had happened. It was so . . . bizarre and scary. Like a scene from 'The Twilight Zone'. Jack, there is more to her than I thought, than any of us thought. And now seeing this about Greg's wife --- who knows what it could be."

Jack looks over the papers again. He doubts Julie knows she's adopted, not seeing the way she acts around Karen and Eve. *But if this is a secret, why would Karen risk it coming out be sending for these documents? Unless she's planning* . . . "That's it, it must be."

"What must be?"

"She's planning to tell Julie the truth." *And if she does, and Julie freaks, Greg will choose to stand by her.* "Does she keep more papers at home?"

"Of course, she works from home."

"I need to see them, discreetly."

Denise frowns. "I don't know if I can make that happen. What else do you expect to find?"

"I don't know . . . but I bet this is just the tip."

✳✳✳✳

Returning to the Halloran mansion, Greg decides to spend some time with their son. The news of her secret adoption has, in some ways, hit him as hard as it has Julie. So as he enters the nursery, Julie takes a deep, confidence-building breath and walks up to another door. She can smell the paint on the other side. The aroma is slight, but it's unmistakable. A quick rap on the door and she is invited inside.

Agnes is in the parlor of her suite, sipping tea with Julie's mother. The aging artist has been staying at the mansion while her fabled home --- a former sugar house transformed into a colorful, three-dimension work of art --- undergoes important repairs. In the meantime, Agnes has converted much of her space here into a microcosm of that little world: scattered across the room are mementos of her many adventures and encounters with the great and near-great; paintings in various stages of completion lean against walls and furniture. Sitting on an easel is her current project, a folk art rendering of Faraway Hill's iconic main square.

Julie wills herself not to express anything on her face. The last thing she wants right now is to upset Eve. "Hey, Mom, are you okay?"

Her mother responds with a tired, but calm smile. "We've just been chatting," Agnes explains.

"I have been hearing a <u>very</u> interesting story about Andy Warhol and a certain film he tried to make."

"I'm sure; here are the papers you wanted." She hands the file, the one with the will and life insurance, to her mother. The other one is sitting a few feet away, in another suite, next to Julie's bed.

"Thanks, Julie, I really appreciate it. Agnes, if you don't mind, it's late and we have a big day tomorrow."

"Of course, Eve; just remember that I am here any time." The Eve gives the older woman a light kiss on the cheek, making Julie realize the mother-daughter relationship they've developed. *I need to keep that in mind.*

The moment Eve closes the door behind her; Agnes announces "something is bothering you."

"What makes you say that?"

"Young lady, you don't get to be my age and not learn to read people. Hell, I knew Rock Hudson was gay at first glance. Something has happened today. What was it?"

"I . . . found out something, something about my mother."

"And that is?"

"That's okay, Agnes. I'm fine."

"Does that 'something' also have to do with your Aunt Karen?"

She knows! How the fuck did she find out? "You know Karen is my mother?"

"I know Karen gave birth to you; Eve is your mother."

"How did you ---."

"Your mother confided in me several months ago. She was worried Karen would tell you. How did you find out?"

"When Greg and I went looking for the life insurance, we found my birth certificate and adoption papers."

"I'm sure you have many thoughts going through your head, but I have an important piece of advice for you."

"And that is?"

"Leave things as they are. A mother isn't simply the woman who gives birth to you. She's the one who changes your diapers, walks you to class on the first day of school, guides you through your first period and explains about boys. Eve has been all those things to you."

"I know . . . and I understand what you're saying, but I . . . I still need time."

"Of course; just remember I am here for you, too." Grateful, Julie realizes something else: she and this delightful and wise lady has not only become a mother to Eve, but a grandmother to her.

✱ ✱ ✱ ✱

Richard is late coming home. He is very late.

Ann called his Concord office, but he already left after a day filled with meetings. "I'm sorry Mrs. Davis," the young intern said. "He's been in and out. Have you tried his cell?" She has, twice, and both times it went to voicemail.

It worries her. Of course, she has plenty of time to worry. Growing up, Ann Gale dreamed of being one of the idle rich. Now that she is, the realization hits her: to be idle means to have plenty of empty days.

Finally, Richard calls to say he won't be home for dinner. "With Ben gone, there is a lot to do. The governor is trying to decide whether or not to appoint another replacement or just wait for November." It's an excuse he isn't selling well and she isn't buying it.

I've lost him already.

✱✱✱✱

"I feel so lost."

Richard is sitting at a table at the Common Man, nursing a scotch. Normally when he comes to this restaurant --- the Concord branch of a popular state-wide chain --- it is to schmooze. But not now, not tonight. Tonight it is nearly closing time and few people are left.

Among those few people is a wizened old gnome of a man. Frank Turner has advised politicians and candidates from New England for over forty years. Every strand of gray hair, every wrinkle, represents an experience or a skill that makes him a formidable presence in Washington. He has come for Ben King's funeral and finds himself sitting here, trying to guide his old friend. "Why is that, why do you feel lost?"

"When Ann first told me about Bradley and his blackmail, my instinct was to stand by her, no matter what. I was determined to be the man, the hero. That's the way I was raised. But when I finally did the deed, arranging for the cash and meeting the prick at his motel, I felt . . . I felt so damned dirty. And everything everyone warned me about Ann came true."

"So, what do you want to do? You're still not legally married. Are you going to leave her?"

"How the fuck can I do that, Frank? Half of New Hampshire, the national press and a dozen of my colleagues came to that wedding. Can you imagine the scandal, the humiliation, if the truth got out?"

"I think you could weather it."

Richard shakes his head. "I'm not so sure."

"Do you still love her; do you still want to marry her?"

These are the questions he has been asking himself since paying off Bradley. They are why he feels so damned lost. "I don't know any more."

✸✸✸✸

Karen St. John is standing at the full-length mirror in her bedroom. She is admiring her new black dress, a simple and tasteful piece she bought yesterday at the Mall of New Hampshire. It suits her well, and is just the thing for a funeral.

This is certainly a good morning for a burial: the sun is already shining bright, bathing the town in warmth. Karen can even hear birds chirping outside her window. *I'm glad*, she thinks to herself without realizing the irony, *I hate depressing funerals*.

A timid knock at the door calls her attention. Denise Sullivan stands there, also dressed in black. Her outfit is a little too snug for Karen's taste, but to each her own. Denise hands her a piece of paper. It is the print out of an email that came late last night from her attorney. "Oh, dear, it looks like my stepchildren are at it again."

"Does this mean you'll be going to New York soon?"

"I suppose so," Karen answers with a frustrated sigh. She needs to come up with a new plan anyway, a new plan to rid herself of Greg Halloran. "But we can deal with that later."

****

Jack is sitting in his --- or, more accurately, Joe's living room --- watching CNN and waiting for the coverage of Ben King's funeral. He's sure the family would have preferred no cameras, but apparently even dead senators have no privacy any more.

Little Jack comes out of the master bedroom. The little boy, still in his pajamas, has been taking on too much. It worries Jack. "How is papa?"

His son shrugs. Joe has been experiencing increasing pain recently. He's also been putting off starting treatment. They argued about it last night but didn't resolve anything. Jack is starting to think that his husband has already given up the fight.

"Jack, maybe you should get dressed. Papa might feel better after some more rest." The boy nods and goes into his own room, closing the door behind him.

CNN's "breaking news" graphic appears on the screen. Jack ups the volume to hear anchor Don Lemon: "Vincent Bologna, the alleged Los Angeles crime boss, has been arrested by federal authorities on charges of racketeering, blackmail and . . ."

Finally some good news. Bologna is Joe's stepfather, who chased his wife's daughter/son across the country until he found Jack. They made a deal a few months ago, that Bologna would leave Joe and Little Jack alone as long as they stayed in New Hampshire. But the fear always remained that the old man would come after them again anyway. CNN switches to video showing Vincent being led in handcuffs out of the Westbrook home.

"Good riddance, fucker," Jack whispers at the screen.

****

They do not bury important people here. This isn't the place. The little cemetery behind the Faraway Hill Unitarian Church is where farmers and mill workers and shopkeepers spend eternity.

Until today.

Today, a group of people dressed in black follow the casket out of the church to the rolling landscape of green and stone. The governor is here, a US Senator is here. Celebrities like Agnes Gabler are here. Important businesspeople from across New Hampshire are here. A group of TV news crews follows the mourners, documenting their grief.

For the first time, someone famous, someone important is being laid to rest among the unknowns.

The men carrying the casket position it above the open grave. In a moment, a device will gently and respectfully lower the box. Pastor Elizabeth leads the mourners to this final place. The deceased's widow, daughter and son-in-law stand near the where the tombstone will be placed. Karen St. John and her personal assistant stand just a few steps behind them, as do Patrick Halloran, Lorene Gale and Vivian Bickel.

"From ashes to ashes," Pastor Elizabeth begins, "dust to dust . . ."

Not everyone who was invited is here. Joan Halloran and her son are in Boston, for the latter's graduation from prep school.

But there is one uninvited guest. He is standing several feet away, behind a large elm tree. Dressed in black, Mark Bradley watches silently as his father is laid to rest.

****

Julie's father has been laid to rest. It's comforting in a way to know that this ritual is behind them. She and the others are back at the Halloran mansion. The reception is being held in the opulent, oval Blue Room. A little buffet has been set-up and her mother, sitting in an antique chair, receives the condolences of people she knows and people she doesn't.

Once Lorene Gale has shared a few tears with her friend, Julie gently asks to step out with her for a moment. Both Greg and Ann glance at the two women as they leave, each for a different reason.

Julie leads Lorene into the next door Green Room. This room is smaller, square shaped and, of course, the color green dominates the décor. But this is the closest and most private place. Julie just can't wait any more, despite the advice of Agnes and her husband. "Lorene, I have something very important to talk about."

"Oh, is something wrong with Ann?"

When isn't there something wrong with Ann? Julie shakes her head. "No, it's about me --- and you. I guess I'll just come right out and say it: I know that I'm Karen's daughter and that you probably know it, too."

Shocked, Lorene catches her breath. "How did you find out?"

"Greg and I went to my parents' house yesterday, to get some estate papers. That's when we came across my birth certificate."

"I see. Have you spoken to your mother --- or to Karen?"

"Not yet; I'm not sure I should, or that I will. But I need to know more. I think you are the only person who can tell me."

"Well, I don't know everything."

"Just, please, tell me what you can."

"It . . . it all happened the night of Lewis' bachelor party. His brother David was there and a few of their friends. Frederick couldn't plan things, so Karen and I volunteered. Lewis just learned that Lilly was pregnant and wanted to make the most of his last moments of freedom. That's how he put it. He and I spent a lot of time together that evening, first just talking and then . . . well, you know.

"One of Lewis' friends was attracted to Karen Scott. I don't blame him, then and now she is a truly beautiful woman. His name was Alexander Mundy. He came from a well-to-do family in Maine; timber, I think. Lewis and Alex were friends from prep school and college. They were inseparable. At the same time Lewis and I snuck off to his suite upstairs, Karen and Alex went someplace but I'm not sure where.

"I found out later that they were seeing each other for weeks. Karen learned she was pregnant a few days after the party; I learned I was pregnant a couple of weeks later. Lewis was willing to claim our baby, but Lilly made such a fuss . . well, we all know how that ended. Karen wanted to marry Alex, but he refused to have anything more to do with her. I never understood why; he seemed so drawn to her."

"Where is Alex now?"

"I don't know; I don't think anyone does. After his parents died, he just disappeared."

****

The morning transforms into afternoon and guests begin leaving the mansion. They each take turns giving their final condolences to Eve. The widow sits next to her sister on a settee in the Blue Room. Both are in tasteful black dresses, but Karen's outfit is by far much more glamorous. Some people have been talking as much about her as about Ben. Ann Davis wonders how Eve feels about that, but she doesn't say anything.

Eventually Ann and Richard are among the last guests. Her mother left a few minutes ago, after yet another lengthily talk with Julie. "I wonder what that's all about," she says to her husband.

"Probably nothing," he answers accepting another scotch from the maid. That's his fourth drink today. "Didn't you once say she lost her parents young? I'm sure she's just offering Julie some support."

Ann nods. *He may be right.*

"By the way, I have to leave for Washington tonight."

"So soon, why?"

"Ben's death means I'm the state's only senator again. There is a lot to do."

"Then I'll go with you."

"The apartment's too small. Besides, I'll be busy at the office and at meetings and hearings. Its better you stay here."

There it is, she realizes. *He's pushing me away.* "How long will you be gone?"

"I'm not sure," he shrugs emptying his glass and looking around the room for the maid. "I need a refill."

✳✳✳✳

Once Karen and the Davis' have left, Julie and Greg try to convince Eve to spend another night at the mansion. But she politely declines and returns home.

Home; the place she and Ben all but built from scratch. The place where they raised a daughter, pursued their careers and celebrated birthdays and anniversaries and Christmases. It has always been filled with so much life, whether it was a giddy teenager and her slumber parties or a husband and wife sharing romantic evenings. But now everything is different, everything has changed.

Above the fireplace is a family portrait. Eve can't help but stand there, staring at it. Julie had just turned 15 and starting to blossom into the wonderful young woman she is today. Eve still looks surprisingly young, even to herself. No gray hair, few wrinkles. But it's Ben who stands out: handsome, with a confident smile and brilliant eyes. He was then and remains now the charming young lawyer she fell in love with.

But this is just an empty house now. Its sole owner rests her head against the mantle and begins to cry.

****

Ann is fighting back tears. After the funeral, she and Richard drove home in silence. The maid had already packed a bag; they didn't even get out of the car. She then drove him to the airport, again in silence. He almost didn't kiss her goodbye.

Not wanting to return to a big, empty house, Ann first drives aimlessly through Manchester. The city is back to normal since the fire, although its sad to see the remains of King's Korner all boarded up. It almost looks like a building that had been bombed during a war.

She considers going to her mother's house. Lorene might have some advice. Ann takes the highway up to Faraway Hill, but even as she takes the exit she reconsiders. She and Vivian are planning their own wedding; do they really need to hear about her failed marriage?

So Ann spends a good ten minutes aimlessly driving through town. Faraway Hill is largely shut for the night; even the tourists are staying in. Without thinking about it much, she steers the car a few blocks from the main square. Peter Brandt still lives with his parents; they need him. Both his mom and dad are not well. So, except for his stint volunteering overseas, he hasn't left them.

The Brandt home is a simple, one-story house. It doesn't have a specific architectural style, at least none that Ann can recognize. She sees Peter's car in the driveway and a few lights on. She parks, gets out and walks up the little cement path. The front door is open; this is, after all, a warm night in a small town. Better to leave the door open than run an expensive air conditioner. She knocks. No one answers. "Mr. Brandt, Mrs. Brandt?" Ann peers through the screen. The lights are on but no one answers. She can hear, in the distance, the sound of a shower. Without a concern, she opens to screen door and looks around. No one is here. Down the hall, the shower shuts off. "Mrs. Brandt, are you here? It's Ann."

"They've gone to see my aunt in Claremont."

Ann turns to see Peter, standing outside the bathroom. A towel is wrapped around his waist. The first thing she notices is how much his body has changed since high school. Back then he had few muscles and was a little scrawny, still more boy than man. But not now. Playing on the college baseball team, backpacking in foreign countries and the rigors of policing have altered him. A man stands before her, a handsome, physically impressive young man.

"Ann, is everything okay?"

Crying she runs up to him. "No, Peter, its not. Everything is falling apart." He wraps her in his warm, hard and slightly damp arms. The shower has left him with a clean, refreshing smell. "I've already lost him."

The towel becomes loose during their hug, dropping to the floor. They both know it, but they both say nothing. Instead, Ann lifts her head up, bringing her lips to Peter's. The kiss begins tentatively, hesitantly, until it becomes more impassioned. Without considering anything or anyone else, she takes his hand in hers and leads him naked to his room.

"Ann, are you sure . . ."

She quiets him with another kiss, this time longer and deeper. There's no going back now.

****

Everyone is gone and the mansion is quiet. Greg and Julie are alone in the nursery, mother holding her sleeping child.

"I take it you spoke to Lorene."

Julie nods. "She told me everything she could. My father was someone named Alexander Mundy. He was supposed to be a good friend of Lewis'. Does his name sound familiar?"

"A little; I'll need to think about it. Maybe there'll be something in Dad's study."

"Lorene got pregnant the night of Lewis' bachelor party. Karen was already pregnant but found out a few days after the party. Lilly learned about her pregnancy a week before the party. That's why our birthdays are so close together."

"Does she know what happened to this Alexander Mundy?"

Julie shakes her head. "You know something? Despite all of the lies, all of the secrets, I still love them; all three of them. I had a wonderful childhood. There was so much love and support. My dad --- Ben --- was the greatest person I've ever known."

They are interrupted by Frederick, who explains that "there is a Lt. Tracey from the Manchester Police who needs to speak to Mr. Halloran. He says that it's urgent" Julie and Greg exchange worried looks; *could it be about the fire?* Greg leaves the room to take the call as Julie once again looks into the warm, peaceful face of their son. She gently places him back in the crib, where he snores a little.

When Greg returns she immediately sees pain on his face. *Something else went wrong.* "Greg, what is it?"

"Joe Westbrook died tonight."

EPISODE THREE

Julie insists on knowing the details. She joins Greg in the hall where he holds the phone so they can both hear Aaron Tracey explain what happened.

The end came much faster than anyone expected. Jack and Little Jack had come home from a trip to the grocery store. They found Joe unconscious in the living room, apparently having blacked out from the pain. While their scared and crying son tried to wake his poppa, Jack made a hurried call to 911. Aaron had just come off duty when he saw the ambulance pull up to their building and Jack emerge. The officer followed them to Elliott Hospital, calling his fiancé Chloe on the way. Joe was gone by the time they arrived. "That's part of the cruelty of ovarian cancer," they were told. "Usually the patient will hang on for months or even a year. But not always."

Greg thanks him and promises to call Jack. The moment he hangs up the phone, Julie whispers, "that poor little boy."

****

Ann slowly opens her eyes. She's in a strange bed in a strange room. It takes her a moment to get her bearings.

Peter is next to her, lying on his stomach and snoring lightly. She gently caresses his warm back. Last night was remarkable. It was so very different from the quick, furtive fucks they had in his car back in high school. Maybe it's because they are older, more experienced, but the passion was incredible. From the expert way he sucked her tits to the powerful thrusts of his cock, this is no teenager. This is a man.

Looking around her, though, Ann realizes that this is a man sleeping in a teen's room. This is something that hasn't changed since they were kids. The sports trophies still sit on the home-made shelf on one wall, next to a Faraway Hill High School pennant. Posters of race cars and scantily clad models still adorn another. He still leaves clothes in piles on the floor.

And, still, Peter blissfully snores. She smiles at him. It feels good to be with him again. This is the first time they've ever spent an entire night together. Back in school, they each had to go home right away.

That's went it hits her: home. Home is now in Concord. *Shit, what have I done?*

****

It took forever for Little Jack to fall asleep. He was hysterical all night, crying, screaming, throwing things. Aaron and Chloe, stayed with them through it all. Finally the boy wore himself out and is now in his room.

Jack is lying on the sofa, eyes closed. He hasn't really slept. *I can't believe he's gone.* The doctors were surprised, too. Everyone was expecting the cancer to be lingering, emotionally draining them for months. *What the fuck am I going to do?*

A knock; Jack rises quickly. Aaron and Chloe are asleep in the master bedroom and he doesn't want to wake them. He opens the apartment door to see Greg standing there. Without saying a word, the two men embrace. They spoke briefly last night, and Jack is glad to see him. "Does Julie know you're here?"

"Yeah and she's being really cool about it. Of course, she just lost her own dad, so she understands what Little Jack is going through."

They stand there, at the threshold, holding each other.

****

Denise finds Mrs. St. John having her usual breakfast of croissants. The living room hasn't been refurnished yet. The decorator is scheduled to drive in from Boston tomorrow.

Mrs. J's eerie calm again sends a chill up Denise's spine. "Good morning."

Looking up the refined lady can see her young assistant is nervous and trying to hide something. *Shit, how can I keep her from finding what I know?*

"What's wrong, dear?"

"What makes you think something is wrong?"

"It's written all over your face."

"Well . . ." Denise grasps for what she hopes will be an easy answer. "A friend of mine passed away last night." She had gotten a text this morning from Jack about Joe's death. She called him shortly after "Someone I met in Manchester a few months ago."

"A young man, I suppose."

"Yes, ma'am."

"I'm very sorry."

"Thank you."

"I suppose there will be a funeral."

"I suppose."

"Well, I need to go to New York. Please make the necessary arrangements."

"Do you want me to go with you?"

"No, dear, not right away. After your friend's funeral."

"Thank you, Mrs. St. John."

****

Lorene Gale is sitting on her back porch, enjoying the cool breeze on a warm morning. So much is going right for her these days: Munroe is at peace; Ann is happily married; the farm is doing well and Vivian is a permanent part of her life. But into this idyll came Julie Halloran and her questions. They've brought up memories Lorene was sure she could set aside.

"Penny for your thoughts."

Lorene looks up to see Vivian, standing beside her, smiling. She is holding a tray carrying two glasses of iced tea. "Is something wrong, Lorene?"

"No, not wrong . . . I don't think. Julie Halloran found out she's adopted."

"How did that happen? I thought that fact was buried long ago."

Lorene takes a glass from the tray. "She and Greg stumbled on her adoption papers at Eve's house."

"I suppose she asked you about Alex." Vivian sits in the chair next to her. "Did you tell her?"

Lorene takes a sip and nods. "I'm surprised at how well she took the news. But I don't think Eve or Karen are aware what she knows."

"What makes you say that?"

"Just the way they were acting. They're bound to find out sooner or later. I guess we'll just have to see what happens then."

****

Greg is gone to see Jack. Johnny has had his morning feeding. Agnes is busy painting. For the first time since learning the truth about her parents, Julie has the freedom to do some research. She is now sitting in Lewis' study, at his computer, keying in the name "Alexander Mundy" into Google.

There are several references to an old 1960s TV show starring Robert Wagner. None of this helps her. So, she refines the search as "Mundy Family Maine".

Some articles appear, mostly from the online archives of the *Portland Press-Herald*. The Mundy family was once quite prominent, primarily in timber and fishing. Like the Hallorans, they date back to colonial days. The family arrived in the Americas from Derbyshire a generation earlier. Portland and the area around it have several markers reflecting the family's influence, like street names. There is even a building in city's historic Old Port District named Mundy House. It has a restaurant inside.

But its one headline above all others that gets Julie's attention: "Mundy Family Tragedy". The article is dated more than twenty years ago. It's the shocking story of George Mundy, his wife and two daughters dying in a plane crash. Only his son Alexander survived.

Another article, from a month later, details the surprising discovery that the Mundy family's timber business had been mortgaged to finance a failed new line of cargo ships. Alex was wiped out.

And that is the last article. It's as if Alexander Mundy has disappeared. No matter which search engine Julie uses --- Google, Yahoo, Bing --- the result is the same. *What the hell happened to him?*

****

The simple, three story red brick building sits on Bridge Street in downtown Manchester. There is nothing really remarkable about it. Most people driving past its green awning and plate glass windows don't know it, but inside are the corporate offices of the Atlantic-New Hampshire Bank.

A cars pulls up to the lot behind it; parking in its designated spot among those of other executives. Eve King turns off the engine. Instead of opening the door, she just sits. When burying her husband yesterday, Eve's boss told her to "take your time" before coming back to work. But spending less than one day alone in her big, empty house convinced Eve that she needs the distraction.

Unfortunately, there is one thing she forgot: the view through her windshield. Not far away is Brady-Sullivan Plaza, where Ben once had his law office. For years, she parked in this spot knowing that her great love is only a short walk away. There was always a comfort in seeing that skyscraper so close. They often met for lunch somewhere near Elm Street or ran into each other as both walked to or from a meeting. Seeing that tower used to make her smile.

Today, it makes her cry.

****

Greg has never seen Jack cry before. Jack is always the cool, confident and often cocky dude who can handle any situation. He's been that way ever since Greg has known him. But today is different. For half an hour, he tearfully describes the traumatic evening. "He'd been sleeping most of the day, but that seemed okay . . . he told us he'd be fine, so Jack and I went to get something for dinner . . . when we came back, he was passed out right here, where we're sitting . . . ."

"I was promised more time . . . they said he'd go slowly, that's the way it normally happens, losing him a piece at a time . . . but that's not what happened. What the fuck am I going to do now?"

The other guests, the cop who called Greg last night and his fiancée, emerge from the bedroom. Jack recovers himself long enough to make introductions. "They've been great to us, Greg, really cool, really helpful."

Chloe volunteers to make some coffee. Aaron asks what should be done now. Jack shrugs, "I guess call his mom and start making arrangements."

****

"It looks like I am going to have to make some new arrangements."

Julie has stopped by Agnes' suite to see if the dear old lady is in need of anything. At least, that's her official reason. The truth is she likes spending time with her. "What arrangements are those, Agnes?"

"That artists' conference coming up at the Mount Washington Hotel; I'm suppose to speak. But Scarlet isn't sure she can escort me and my grandson is much too young for that kind of responsibility."

"Well, I'm sure something can be worked out. Can I ask you something?"

"Of course, what is it?"

"Do you know anything about a family named Mundy?"

"Mundy? Oh, hell, yes. Old man George Mundy was such an ass, just like his father. Both were very arrogant, sure he knew what was best. In reality neither of them really had much in the way of brains, especially when it came to business. That's what ruined the family. Well, that and the awful accident."

"The plane crash, you mean."

"Yes, and that left poor Alex all alone. And broke, too, from what I understand. I wonder what happened to him."

"Don't you know?"

"I don't think anyone does. He seemed to disappear right after the funeral. Why do you ask?"

"Last night, I cornered Lorene Gale. She told me that Alex Mundy is my father."

"I see . . . well, he was quite the ladies' man. Is she certain?"

Julie nods. "I went online this morning but there isn't much about him. Like you said, he's pretty much dropped off the face of the earth."

Agnes studies her. "Young lady, you've taken in quite a bit in a very short amount of time."

"I know."

"You need a break so that you can get your bearings. Come to the conference with me. You won't have to do much; it can be a vacation for you."

"Oh, I don't know Agnes. I've never left Johnny alone before."

"Johnny will not be alone; he has his father and his nanny. Bretton Woods is so beautiful this time of year. Have you ever been to the Mount Washington?"

"No, but . . ."

"Then it's settled."

✳✳✳✳

"Are you all settled, sir?"

Mark Bradley loves sitting in First Class. He enjoys the roomy seats, the special service and especially the flight attendants. Smiling at him right now is a hot little redhead in a nicely snug uniform that packages her tits nicely. "Sure, kid, and thanks."

Looking out his window, he can see the Manchester International Airport move farther and father away as the plane taxis to the runway. In little over an hour he'll be back in New York, living the cushy life he deserves.

Best of all, he will be able to put Faraway Hill behind him. The place has served its purpose and Mark doubts he'll ever come back.

But you never know.

****

When she hears "please explain to your mother," the irony is not lost on Denise.

Mrs. St. John is sitting in an exquisite chair beside an exquisite little desk in her exquisitely decorated bedroom. Even the silk robe she's wearing is exquisite. She is talking on her cell to Julie Halloran. "Have you spoken to her today?"

Denise is packing Mrs. J's clothes for her trip back to New York and every time she reaches into the closet her eyes can't help but gaze at the little package on the shelf.

"Well, she <u>did</u> say she was going back to work . . . nonsense, it's probably the best therapy . . . it'll keep her mind off Ben . . . dear, it's her way of coping . . . of course you should go . . . the Mount Washington is a magnificent place and you really need the vacation, especially after losing so much . . . thank you dear, and we'll talk again when I get back. Love you."

Mrs. J. closes her cell and looks at Denise with a contented smile. "Be sure to include a couple of really good dresses; I expect to go to a few parties while I'm there."

****

This is not the graduation party that Patrick Halloran wanted.

He planned on going out with some of his buds, hitting the bars of Harford and maybe score for themselves a few hot ladies. It would be one last night to go wild. There is a particular girl he's had his eye on, and Patrick knows where she'll be partying tonight. But all of this wishing is pointless; instead, he is having an early dinner with his aunt and cousin. They are going to a concert afterward. Its something he can't get out of, so Patrick sits here and smiles politely.

"We're all very proud of you," Aunt Joan beams, as if she were his mother. Sadly his real mother cannot be here; she is in a personal care facility miles away.

"Thanks," Patrick answers while noticing what looks like a few new tucks around her eyes. She takes a few bites of her salmon salad.

They are dining at Carbone's, a popular restaurant in Hartford not too far from the Yale campus. It's an elegant, family-owned place with arched ceilings and warm colors.

"And congrats to you, dude" He says to Joan's son, Matthew, who graduated from prep school yesterday. The boy smiles shyly. "Thanks." Matthew is sitting between his mother and her latest husband (number four), a former model not too many years older that her son. Paul Lansing has the same bewildered look Patrick always sees.

Actually, if there were any family he'd like tonight --- other than his mother --- it would be his cousin Greg and Greg's wife, Julie. He likes them both and both are only a few years older than himself. But they are dealing with her dad's sudden death. He'll be seeing them in a few days, when he moves permanently to Faraway Hill and takes a full-time position in the family company.

"I'm sure you'll love the concert tonight," Joan says. "I'm one of the symphony's patrons, you know."

"I can't wait, Aunt Joan," Patrick answers with another forced smile.

✷✷✷✷

"I can't wait too much longer, Frank. I need to make a decision soon."

Frank Turner's wrinkled old face adds some more creases as he ponders his friend's dilemma.

Richard and Frank are back in DC; Richard flew in last night and Frank returned this afternoon. When Frank arrived he noticed two things: the rest of the staff is gone, and Richard has been drinking. It looks like he's been drinking one-and-off for hours.

"Maybe I should just cut my losses, and let her go."

"You just told me yesterday that you were afraid of the scandal."

Richard empties his glass. "Yes, but if I do it right away . . . I mean, Frank, my term isn't up for another two years." He notices the bottle is empty, so he opens up a cabinet to look for another. "That should be enough time to recover. Hell, you told me yourself I should be able to weather this."

"You need to think about this some more."

He finds a bottle of scotch toward the back and brings it out. "I've been doing plenty of thinking."

****

Ann spends the day thinking about her situation. Or, more accurately, trying not to think about it.

She quietly left the house while Peter remained sleeping. He's called her three times since, and all three times she sends it to voicemail.

First, she drove to Manchester where she had a quick bagel and coffee. She strolled down Elm Street, again noticing the sad sight of a boarded up King's Korner. By mid morning, she was window shopping at the Mall of New Hampshire where she had lunch in the food court.

Everywhere she goes, people recognize her. They are not discrete; Ann can hear the whispers "that's Ann Halloran" and "that's Ann Davis" several times. When she stops in Macy's to browse, a sales associate steps right up and say "let me know if you need anything, Mrs. Davis."

Ann isn't sure if this means she's still New Hampshire's most scandalous woman, or if she is now the respected wife the state's senator.

Whatever people think, her mind keeps going back to Richard and Peter and how confusing the situation is. But it's when she overhears a mother and daughter's private conversation that another thought crosses Ann's mind: and it frightens her. *Oh my God, could it be?*

She considers her options. But everyone knows her. If Ann makes the purchase herself, the word will get out fast. She can just see the headlines in both the *Union Leader* and the *Concord Monitor*. That's the last thing she or Richard need.

Driving back to Concord, a plan starts to form. She parks on North Main Street and strides up to the city's premier pharmacy, the Prescription Center. The Davis' have been using it for years. If anyone can be discrete, it's the shop's staff. One of the resident pharmacists emerges just as Ann arrives at the door. "Hello, Mrs. Davis."

"Hello Cathy; I'm glad to run into you. I'm hoping you can do me a favor."

"Well, I'm supposed to have dinner with my husband and Perry's waiting for me."

"This won't take long." In low tones, Ann explains what she needs. Everything is done in less than three minutes and Ann is back in her car, driving to Four Corners.

Once inside, she immediately heads up to the master bedroom. A quick read of the instructions and a few minutes later come the result.

The test is positive.

EPISODE FOUR

Ann can tell that it's going to be a hot and humid day. Even this early in the morning, she can feel the warmth of the sun and thickening of the air. There will certainly be alerts for people with breathing problems.

She has just parked her car a discrete distance from her destination. Ann hopes to draw as little attention as possible. Faraway Hill, like all small towns everywhere, trades in gossip. And since last year's scandals involving Munroe and Mark, people especially love to gossip about her.

Dr. Phelps runs his family practice from a converted house a few blocks from the main square on what is appropriately called Apothecary Road. The former home is warm and charming and welcoming, with a porch and stain glass windows. The Phelps' have been serving the people of Faraway Hill for three generations from this building. And a fourth is coming: Dr. Phelps daughter, who went to high school with Ann and Julie, is away getting her medical degree.

"Well, hello little Annie Gale."

Ann smiles at the nurse, a friendly gray haired woman who has worked here since Ann can remember. "Dr. Phelps is expecting you." The nurse leads her to an exam room. Unlike most clinics today, this room is anything but cold and clinical. The woodwork is painted a soft cream and the wallpaper is a fading rose pattern.

The door opens and a smiling Dr. Phelps enters. Other than Ben's funeral, it has been several months since she saw him. He hasn't changed much since; but, then, other than some graying at the temples, he hasn't changed much since she was a teen either. "Good morning Ann."

"Good morning doctor."

"I don't normally see patients this early. What's the big emergency?"

Ann tells him about the home pregnancy test. He agrees to confirm the results. It doesn't take long to obtain the sample, but waiting for a final answer seems excruciating to her. She needs to know for certain and immediately. Finally, the doctor returns with an even bigger smile.

"Congratulations, young lady: you are going to be a mother."

****

Things should be easier now. At least, that's what Patrick Halloran hopes as he pulls his car up under the portico. He's been living an itinerant life the last several months. Patrick has been on the road so much that he barely saw the furnished apartment he'd been renting in New Haven.

But now he is taking up permanent residence at the family homestead. Although Patrick isn't sure how well he'll adapt to small town life. "You'll do fine," his mother said over the phone this morning. "Just give it time." It worries him how weak her voice has become. Fortunately, Faraway Hill is a fairly short drive to her personal care home in Concord.

"Welcome, Mr. Halloran," Fredrick the aging butler greets him. The old man directs a couple of maids to help carry luggage upstairs to the suite Patrick has been using. These rooms will be his from now on. Greg lived in here before his marriage and until recently there were still mementos of his cousin's youth scattered about. They have now been removed and Patrick can start personalizing the space.

School is over; now his life really begins.

****

"Dude, I thought school was supposed to be over."

Billy Grant is Matthew Newberry's fellow plebe at the Brothers. They have just emerged from a study session in the lodge's vast, mahogany-lined library.

"It's not so bad."

"Maybe for you; not for me." Billy has been having a tough time with his indoctrination and initiation. Of course, he is also is under a lot of pressure: not only has his family been Brothers for generations, but both his father and older brother are important members. "I mean the sex part I'm getting the hang of. It's all these fucking rules and history we have to learn."

Oddly enough, it's been just the opposite for Matthew. He understands the argument, that being intimate binds the Brothers together, but sex with other guys is just something he would never do otherwise. "You'll get it," Matthew tells him. "Just be patient."

"Sure; anyway, I've got door duty this afternoon." As plebes, they do much of the menial work in the lodge. That's part of being low on the totem pole. Matthew is scheduled to work the dining room tonight.

As Billy walks over to the foyer, Matthew climbs the ancient the staircase up to his room where he finds a note from his tutor, Justin, which reads simply "we need to talk."

****

"We need to talk."

Ann has spent another day driving around aimlessly, trying to figure out what to do. She skipped lunch, avoided people. As evening comes, she realizes she has only one option. So she is now standing in Peter's office in the cinder block building that houses the Faraway Hill Unified Police Force.

"Are you sure, Ann?" he asks, barely looking up from the paperwork on his desk. "I've been calling you for two days and you just ignore me."

"Peter ---"

"Is making love to me that fucking awful?"

He's hurt and he's angry; Ann understands that. But he needs to understand her, too, so she states simply and directly "I'm pregnant."

Not expecting to hear this, Peter just stops and stares silently at her.

"I'm about six weeks along. I realized yesterday that I missed my period, so I saw Dr. Phelps this morning. It's actually kind of ridiculous, that it should be such a surprise. My cycle is so regular you can set a watch to it. Now, Julie, her cycle can be all over the road ---"

"Have you told Richard yet?"

Ann shakes her head.

"Are you going to tell him?"

"Of course; it'll probably save our marriage."

Peter clucks in disbelief, as if he's dealing with a nutty female. "Fuck, Ann, that's asinine. He's obviously having second thoughts and this will just make him feel trapped."

"No, he'll give me a second chance now."

"And what about me, what about us?"

"Peter, please ---"

"Sorry, I forgot: just like in high school. If I wasn't good enough for Ann Gale, the farmer's daughter, I'm sure as hell not good enough for Ann Halloran, the senator's wife."

"Peter ---"

"Go. Now. Please."

✼✼✼✼

Julie planned to spend the day out in the garden with her son. She wants to spend as much quality time with him as possible. But it's been too humid. So they've stayed inside the house, relaxing in the family room on the first floor. "We should be grateful," Frederick explains, "to Mr. Halloran's grandparents."

"Why is that?"

"They had installed air conditioning during the renovation. Forgive me for saying so, madam, but the house was often bloody unbearable during the summer before then."

"I can imagine." The mention of family has Julie thinking about her own convoluted circumstance. Cradling little Johnny in her arms, his sweet smile and innocent eyes are about the only simple things in her life. This evening she will explain to Greg about her trip with Agnes, and call her mother as well.

✼✼✼✼

Some habits linger. Eve King awoke this morning thinking that she needs to get Ben's coffee ready. One glance at the empty side of the bed brought her back to reality.

Being back at the office is helping. During the day she again forgets what happened. Twice she found herself reaching for the phone to call her husband.

Now, home for the evening, it's easy to imagine that he's simply in Washington. But he's not. He's gone forever. *God, how I miss you.*

The door bell brings Eve out of her reverie. Opening it she finds her sister Karen, as stylish as always, with an oddly cheerful smile as if all is right with the world. *She's in Karenland again.* "How are you doing, Eve?"

"I'm just fine, Karen. Everything is fine. Is that why you are here?"

"Partially; I do worry so about you."

I'll bet. "What is the other reason?"

"I must fly to New York." Karen sweeps past her and into the living room. "There are some matters involving the St. John Group that I have to deal with personally. I don't know how long I'll be gone."

"That's fine, and there's no reason for you to rush back."

Karen raises a carefully sculpted eyebrow. "And what does that mean?"

"It means the farther you are from Julie the better."

"She's <u>my</u> daughter."

Eve comes very close to slapping her baby sister when the phone rings. Seeing the number of the caller ID, she picks up the receiver. "Hello, Julie."

"How are you holding up, Mom?"

"Just fine."

"I hate that you are all alone over there. Are you sure you don't want to stay here at the mansion?"

"No, Julie. In fact, your Aunt Karen came over to keep me company."

"I'm glad. Anyway, I'm also calling to tell you that I'm going out of town for awhile. Agnes has this artist conference up at Bretton Woods. But since Scarlet has been called away I've volunteered to go with her."

"That's sounds like a wonderful idea. I'm sure that you can use the break."

"I think so too; love you."

"I love you too." With a sense of victory, Eve sets the phone down and turns to Karen. "<u>My</u> daughter is going on a trip up north. So thankfully there will be even more distance between you."

"Sister, dear, do you really think that, with Ben gone, we can keep the truth a secret?"

Eve walks back to the front door, opens it, and says simply, "have a safe trip."

****

Greg isn't sure why he chose Maxwell's for dinner. It was the first thing that came to his mind when inviting Jack and his son. After hanging up, Greg remembers that Maxwell's was the first place in Manchester where he and Jack were alone together. That was well over a year ago.

Photos of historic Manchester line the restaurant's rich mahogany walls. Greg is standing at the entrance admiring a huge image of the grand old Amoskeag Bank building when he hears, "Hey there, handsome; long time no see."

Greg turns to see Debbie, one of the staff and a girl he fucked for awhile after first returning home from NYU. She was a great lay, and a lot of fun. But when she seemed to get serious he cooled things off between them. It was about that time he started dating Julie King and took advantage of Mark Bradley's rumored services.

The sight of her also reminds him how long it's been since he last had sex with anyone. Debbie is wearing her tight uniform, which accentuates her tits and round ass. Months have past, and he's starting to feel it. Seeing her again even gets him a little hard. "Hey, Deb, how are things?"

"Same; nothing much changes for me. Are you alone tonight?"

"I'm meeting Jack and his son here."

"His son? Is that the little boy I've seen him around town with?"

"Yeah."

"I thought the other guy was his dad."

"Well, sort of."

A curious smile crosses Debbie's face. Thankfully, Jack and Little Jack arrive at this moment, keeping her from asking the inevitable. After introductions, she leads the trio past a row of booths. Each has high mahogany seats and walls that effectively create little alcoves. Greg knows he promised Julie to keep his meetings with Jack discrete; but he doubts that she'll begrudge them a dinner together.

Debbie leaves them at a booth with some menus (and a wink to Greg).

"So guys," Greg asks them, knowing he sounds forced, "how are you holding up?"

Little Jack says nothing. He just stares at the pictures in his menu.

"Not bad," says the boy's father. "But, of course, we miss Papa." Little Jack silently nods.

"I'm sure."

"Tomorrow we're picking up Uncle Nick and Grandma at the airport."

"Your mother's coming to the funeral?"

Nick shakes his head. "No, Joe's mother; my mom can't make it. But Jack's looking forward to seeing his grandmother, aren't you?"

Once again, the little boy just nods. Jack looks worried. When Greg spoke to him earlier in the day, he explained how withdrawn Little Jack has become. "He's not acting like himself, he won't talk to me about his papa or, really, much of anything."

Greg tries to get him to open up. "See anything you like on the menu?"

The boy mere shrugs, so Greg adds "they make great hamburgers here, really thick and juicy. The fries are unbelievable, too."

Little Jack says nothing and Greg realizes that this will be a long, uncomfortable dinner.

✳✳✳✳

Ann silently eats her dinner, all alone, in the dining room at Four Corners.

This is not what I signed up for, she thinks. Growing up Ann always dreamed of a more glamorous life away from the crumbling Gale Farm. Now she has that life, with a big bank account, a fancy home and a respected husband (or almost-husband). And yet, here she is, eating pasta by herself.

Gertrude, the grandmotherly housekeeper and the Davis' only full-time servant emerges from the kitchen. "Would you care for anything else, Mrs. Davis?"

"No Gertrude, but thanks; go and enjoy the movie." Gertrude's grandson is in town from college and wants to spend some time with her. The housekeeper thanks her. Ann listens carefully to make sure she hears the door close. Then, not yet finished with dinner, she pulls out her cell phone and dials.

Richard doesn't pick-up. Instead, it goes right to voicemail. "Sweetheart, this is Ann. We need to talk. It's important. I'm flying to Washington tomorrow. Please make sure we have some time together."

****

"Dude, you need to spend more time with the other plebes."

Matthew is in his assigned bedroom at the Brothers' lodge, where his tutor, Justin Wight, sits next to him on the bed.

"I know Justin, it's just . . . I just can't get into it."

Like everything else in the Brothers' lodge, the bedroom has an aura of age and stability. The furniture is old and heavy. The floor creaks a little when you walk on it. Hanging over the bed is an expensive painting that must have been nailed to the same place for decades.

"These guys are going to be more than friends to you. These are dudes that you will know for the rest of your life, dudes you'll need to trust."

"I know."

"What about Billy Grant? I've seen you hang out with him."

"Yeah, so?"

"So, you do anything with him?"

"Just study together."

"Dude, you need to get more involved. You know what I mean by that. Billy's really into it, I bet he can help."

"Okay, I'll talk to him."

****

People often talk about New York's skyline at night. But there is also a special beauty in viewing it from an airplane window early in the morning. Seeing it again makes Karen smile.

Karen loves the luxury that comes with being Mrs. St. John --- like flying First Class. It's what she dreamed of as a little girl growing up in Keane and Faraway Hill. And, despite some setbacks, applying Daddy's logic has gone a long way to give her the things she wants most in life.

Unfortunately, the money comes with stepchildren.

This is why she has Martin's lawyer pick her up at JFK. Along the way he lays out the problem: Madeline and Jeffrey are claiming that she has essentially abandoned the company by moving back to New Hampshire. "They want to replace you as chairwoman," he explains, "and they've lined up some powerful board members."

Karen has long expected this move, and already has a plan. "Let me tell you what we are going to do."

****

The mountains are made of steel with a matte black finish. Hovering over them and slowly turning are clouds of black, aluminum plates.

Ann is standing in the vast polished marble atrium of the Hart Senate Office Building. On her past visits, she hasn't had much of an opportunity to admire the modernist sculpture. Despite the sharp angles and stark blackness, it is oddly comforting. It reminds her a little of the mountains back home.

"I'm sorry for the delay, Mrs. Davis," the perky young intern says. The girl is about 19, one of many college students working for Richard during the summer. Ann has already forgotten her name.

"That's quite alright."

The girl leads Ann to an elevator and up to Richard's suite. Once there, the place is a beehive of activity. Another intern, this time a young man, welcomes Ann by saying "it's such a crazy morning, but the senator is waiting for you."

Waiting is right. When Ann enters his private chamber she sees him standing by the window, hands clasped in front him, calm and patient. "Good morning," he says formally. No kiss, no hug. *That's not good.*

"Sweetheart, I am so sorry."

"About what?"

"You got more than you bargained for with me."

He doesn't answer, he doesn't even smile.

"But, believe me Richard, I love you. I really do. And I have news."

"What kind of news?"

"I'm pregnant."

Now he reacts, but in shock not in joy. *Oh, my God, no . . .*

"Are you sure?"

"Yes, I saw the doctor yesterday. Please tell me you're happy. I'm happy and so should you."

"I . . . I just never expected to be a father again, at my age."

Ann walks up to him --- nearly running, actually --- and throws her arms around him. "This means a fresh start! It does; I know that it does."

Richard doesn't say anything; he just returns her hug. That's good enough for Ann, who is convinced: *we have a chance.*

✷✷✷✷

As they driver further and further north from Faraway Hill, Julie can feel the stress slowly seep from her pores. It's like the long trek is a cleanser, a form of detox from the complex world back home.

The stories Agnes tells also help. They are funny and revealing and about famous people like Gore Vidal ('what an ego that queen had!") and Marilyn Monroe ("I don't think I ever saw the poor girl happy").

She is also a font of advice. "I don't know what to do about Greg," Julie explains. "On the one hand, he cheated on me and is in love with someone else --- another man at that --- on the other hand, he is always there for me when I need him. Look at how he's stood by me through Dad's death and learning about the adoption."

"Maybe," Agnes counters with a wise smile, "he's a better friend to you than a husband." This is the kind of advice Julie needs. She knows that she can't turn to her two mothers for help. At least not right now.

Another help is letting someone else do the driving. Julie has been using rented limos often since becoming Mrs. Halloran. Before that, her only time in a limo was senior prom. It's a perk she never expected to get used to, but now can't imagine going without.

Coming off the highway, they arrive at a long, winding road that leads the limo through some meadows and a golf course. In the distance are the magnificent White Mountains. Almost immediately the magnificent Mount Washington Hotel comes into view. Nestled at the base of Mt. Washington, the hotel is huge: a giant, opulent white Spanish Renaissance Revival building surrounded by a sea of green. White, that is, except for the stunning roof, made of brilliant red metal roof shimmering under the sun. "Wow" is all Julie can say.

"What until we get inside."

There are other cars, some of them limos, at the main entrance. Looking through her window, Julie can recognize some of the people emerging as familiar faces from TV or magazines. It takes a few minutes but they, too, have their arrival moment. The limo is surrounded by hotel staff who take their luggage from the trunk and help the two women out of the car. The first thing Julie notices is the weather: while still warm, it isn't as humid as back home.

Julie next notices the man. She isn't sure why he, of all the people around them, he should get her attention. Maybe because he is so damned cute; he is a little younger that she, probably just out of college. The man has the lean, fit build of someone who stays active and enjoys it. His eyes sparkle almost as much as the hotel's metal roof and his smile is all charm.

"Hello ladies," he says greeting them. "My name is Eric and I am a management trainee here at the hotel. I have been assigned to assist you during the conference."

Assist is right; for the first time in months Julie actually thinks about sex. She suddenly imagines what the young man must look like naked. *I can't believe this; I'm married with a son --- of course, so is my husband.* She chuckles, causing him to give her a curious look.

Eric escorts them into the lobby. If the exterior is impressive, the hotel's Great Hall --- which is what the lobby is called --- is beyond anything Julie expected. As grand as the Halloran mansion is, the Mt. Washington almost puts it to shame. The Great Hall is a spectacular space with columns rising high above them, large windows and a fireplace with, of all things, a mounted moose above the mantle. In any other hotel, the Great Hall would be the ballroom.

After checking in, Eric personally wheels Agnes toward an ornate elevator. Julie follows them inside where a uniformed operator manipulates the controls. "We've given you ladies the Luxury Family Suite," the young man explains. "We felt that you would be more comfortable there."

Like everything else at the Mt. Washington, what is called the "family suite" is more that its name. It's like a luxurious apartment. There is a large living room with a fireplace, flat screen TV and a private bar. The suite has three bedrooms and one-and-a-half baths. Julie estimates it to be at least a thousand square feet.

A pair of staffers is already here; depositing their luggage and then they quickly depart. "We certainly do hope you enjoy your stay, Miss Gabler and Mrs. Halloran," Eric says with all the courtesy of an eager young professional. "You can reach me any time. The number for my direct line is beside each phone."

Agnes thanks him, but its Julie who notices his well-rounded ass as Eric strolls out the door.

****

"I want you to meet my brother, Nick."

The boy doesn't say anything. He doesn't even look up. Instead, he remains focused on the coloring book Jack bought him.

"Won't you at least say hi?"

Again, nothing.

"It's okay, dude," Nick says, "We've got plenty of time to get to know each other."

They are currently in the VIP lounge at the Manchester International Airport. It was here, more than a year ago, where Jack and the Hallorans met Greg and Julie after Lewis' death. Now Jack is back, because of another man's death; this time the killer is cancer and not a drunken farmer's bullet.

Nick tussles his nephew's hair and sits between father and son. "So, when is she getting here?"

"She was supposed to be here by now, but her flight was delayed." Joe's mother is coming and Jack has mixed feelings about it. He felt obligated to call her with the news and had to hear her sobs over the phone. She insisted on coming to the funeral. But the woman has never accepted Jackie's transformation. "Think about it," Joe once told him. "I have five o'clock shadow, biceps and a penis but she still thinks of me as her little girl."

"What's the news back home?" Jack has been to busy to speak to his mother except with the same sad news. She's sending flowers.

"The old man is practically in a coma. He hasn't said anything in weeks. Mom's a wreck; she wants you to visit and bring Little Jack."

Jack doubts his son is old enough to handle another death scene. "Besides," he explains to his brother, "Dad hates me. He made that clear."

"Dude, he never changed the will."

"What do you mean?"

"Just what I said; Mom kept the lawyer away just long enough for him to cool down. And when we told him about Little Jack, well, that ended that."

This opens up a new scenario: if Greg can't or won't take him back, then Jack can bring his son to New York. Of course, he'd return only after his father's death.

"Grandma!"

The look up to see Little Jack run to the lounge door where his grandmother, eyes red with tears, welcomes him with a kiss and a hug.

****

It's the end of the day. Nearly everyone else has gone home. The Millyard has transitioned from a center of activity to a quite corner of the city.

Of the few people left behind are Greg Halloran and his cousin Patrick. After hours of meetings of one sort or another, the two of them are relaxing in Greg's office. "I hate to tell you," he tells Patrick, "that one of us needs to go to Atlanta soon."

The Hallorans operate a textile mill in Georgia. There are usually mini crisis of one kind or another. Greg's father traveled there often. But Greg has only gone once in the past year. Someone needs to make another trip.

"No problem; I can do it."

"That would be great."

The two men are drinking sparkling water; Greg's father didn't like having alcohol at the office. "I really appreciate all the work you've been doing."

"Hey, dude, it's a family business and we're family."

Greg smiles, nods and takes another drink. Patrick does the same before saying, "so tomorrow's the funeral."

"Yeah."

"Want me to go with?"

"Actually, that would be cool. Thanks."

"How is Jack holding up?"

"Not well. He's worried about his son."

"I'm sure. Any idea, I mean, what happens next?"

"With me and Jack or me and Julie? Damned if I know."

****

There are few restaurants more distinctively New York than Delmonico's. In business on and off (and with several different owners) since the 1830s, people from all over the world come to the handsome triangular stone building for the cuisine and the history inside. Legend has it that the columns from the entrance were imported from the ruins of Pompei. Karen doesn't really believe that; but the tale is one of those that New Yorkers relish.

Delmonico's has a lot of tales, often involving the famous and the infamous such as Teddy Roosevelt, F. Scott Fitzgerald, Oscar Wilde and James "Diamond Jim" Brady. Mark Twain supped here, as did opera legend Jenny Lind.

Karen is sitting in the main dining room, surrounded by many of the city's most important residents. The mayor is a few feet away. Her table is not far from one of the windows, where golden drapes frame a teeming but silent view of William Street. She doesn't mind being alone in this elegant atmosphere; it allows her to be on a stage of sorts, as other people slyly look to see who she is.

"Good evening Karen."

"Good evening Madeline, Jeffrey."

Madeline St. John is about Karen's age, but recently added weight makes her look much older. Her younger brother, Jeffrey, still has the delightfully nervous face of a child. Karen invites them to sit. "What will you have? The steak, perhaps?" Delmonico's is famous for its triangular-shaped short loin cut. "I, myself, have been craving the Lobster Newberg."

"We really are not here to eat with you, Karen," Madeline states emphatically. "Dining with our parents' murderer is not the way my brother and I wish to spend an evening."

Karen merely smiles. Madeline has long suspected the truth, but Daddy's logic has made it impossible for her to prove it. "Let's not rehash that old argument, shall we?"

"We have enough votes to oust you as chairwoman of the St. John Group."

"Oh? I don't know why you bother with the effort."

Madeline clenches her fists in frustration. "Removing you as much as possible from our lives is worth almost anything."

This is just what Karen anticipated; Daddy's logic seldom fails her. "What I mean is that I am ready to sell you my shares in the company."

The siblings exchange surprised looks. "Are you serious?" Jeffrey asks.

"Of course, I am. My life is now in Faraway Hill. My family is there and they've welcomed me with open arms. That is my home."

Within a few minutes, the three of them lay out the rough outline of the deal. The sister and brother leave her, thinking of themselves as victorious. Karen, of course, knows who the real winner is.

****

The audience roars with laughter, almost shaking the chandeliers of the hotel's ballroom. Sitting on the stage, holding court is Agnes Gabler. "Andy was always luring me to his Factory. He always came up with the best excuses." With that she begins yet another tale to amuse and enthrall her audience.

Her audience is impressive. Julie has never met such an interesting and eclectic collection of people. There is the painter from Paris who creates near exact replicas of Degas' works. A sculptor from Denmark builds the most amazing pieces from wire clothes hangers. The Russian performance artist who performs intricate works nude --- with her body painted a brilliant red.

Right now Julie is standing toward the entrance of the room, enjoying the audience almost as much as the audience is enjoying Agnes.

"She's pretty cool, huh?"

Julie turns to see Eric, who has just stepped up next to her. *Damn, he really knows how to fill out that uniform.* "Agnes is probably the most interesting and intelligent person I've ever known."

Eric nods in appreciation. Julie appreciates his charming smile and wonders again what he looks like without the uniform.

"I've been working here for over six months and I still get impressed by the people who come here."

"Well, the Mt. Washington is one of those places in New England that attracts the famous and near-famous."

"True; and your almost royalty."

"Pardon?"

"I mean the Hallorans. You family is like New Hampshire's royal family."

"I'm only a Halloran by marriage."

"Well, I guess I'll always be simple Eric Mundy."

EPISODE FIVE

The thunderous applause made it difficult for Julie to hear him. Or, at least, to hear him correctly; *he couldn't possible have called himself Mundy.* "What did you say?"

"I'll always be simple Eric Mundy."

Oh, my God, he did! Could it be a coincidence? Maybe or maybe not, but before Julie can ask him the two of them are surrounded by a sea of boisterous people leaving the ballroom.

****

The sun has nearly disappeared by the time Ann returns to Four Corners. So has her joy. Richard's muted response to the news has weighed on her throughout the flight home. *Maybe Peter's right,* she thinks; *Maybe Richard did plan on ending things and now feels trapped.*

Gertrude, as usual, has left the house spotless. Everything is in its proper place. Everything that is, except for Ann. *Do I even belong here?*

A large manila envelope sits on the coffee table. It is addressed to Ann Davis. The return address is Richard's lawyer. Her heart sinks: *did he already plan on cutting me loose?* She nervously tears open the envelope. Inside are the final papers, including the decree, from her divorce from Mark. The judge has even decreed that she should be called Ann Halloran.

I can't give this up; I just can't. I've waited too damn long to be rich and important. Nobody will take that from me, not Greg, not Mark and not Richard.

****

"Take it from me, dear, this is more than just coincidence."

Eric disappeared as he and Julie were swarmed by the crowd. As soon as possible, she sought out Agnes and wheeled her into the elevator and up to their suite. Julie couldn't wait to tell her and began explaining what happened almost from the moment they crossed the threshold.

"Do you really think so?"

"Well, the name isn't all that common and the Mundys were once very prominent in New England."

"I've got to talk to him."

"And what will you say? It's best to sleep on it first. He'll be on duty tomorrow. By morning you'll have a better idea of how to approach him."

****

The early morning service in the gothic Ursula Chapel is brief. Chloe talks a little about her growing friendship with Joe. Jack deliberately focuses his comments on the two men's joint love for their son. After finishing, Jack takes him into his arms and the boy cries, really cries, for the first time since that awful night.

Aaron, Denise, Greg, Nick and Patrick are all here. Everyone is wearing dignified black, even Denise, although her cleavage is anything but solemn. They all sit quietly and respectfully. But Marjorie Bologna's sobs can be heard throughout the chapel. Eventually the group follows the casket out to the burial spot. Joe is interred in a gently sloping part of Pine Grove Cemetery. His mother watches and weeps. His son clings to Jack's arm.

Once the service ends, Little Jack wanders over to his Uncle Nick. Jack can't hear what they are talking about, but likes seeing them together.

"I can't believe you did that," comes a barely audible voice. It's Marjorie, who has stepped to his side. "I can't believe you buried my little girl with that
. . . that name in that way."

Jack doesn't know what to say. She doesn't seem to expect an answer and simply walks away.

****

Peter isn't in his office. One of the lieutenants tells Ann that he is probably strolling through the town square. "He likes to start his day that way," the officer explains. "That way he has a good idea of what's going on." And that's where Ann finds him, wearing his uniform, standing in the square near the statute of John Halloran.

"Good morning, Mrs. Davis," he greets her coldly.

"Please, Peter, I really need to talk."

"I don't see what about, since I'm not good enough. Not for you, not for Karen St. John, I guess not for anybody."

"Peter, I still need you as a friend. I don't have many friends. I don't know how to have friends."

"You can have all the friends you want, Ann. You just have to be a good friend to them. But I'm too old to just be your friend or your fuck buddy."

"Oh, Peter, I'm sorry. What can I do?"

"Leave him."

"I can't. He's the father of my child."

"That's not the reason, not the whole reason. You like it, you like being Ann Halloran Davis. You like the posh restaurants and the fancy houses. You even like the scandals. Well, ma'am, I'm just a small town boy whose happy to be a small town boy."

With that, he tips his hat and walks away.

****

Julie is trying not to look nervous. She is sitting alone in the hotel's conservatory, a handsome semi-circular space topped by a high dome ceiling. A waiter brings her an iced tea and a copy of today's *USA Today*. Inside is a brief story of the governor naming her father's replacement in the US Senate.

My father: she and Agnes talked about Eric this morning. "You need to be very tactful," Agnes advised her before the convention started. "He may not be the Mundy you think. And if he is, I'm sure he's not expecting a big sister he never knew to suddenly show up."

When Eric arrives, he gives her his best professional smile. Julie realizes how creepy it is now to think of him sexually. "You wanted to see me Mrs. Halloran. Is everything alright?"

"Yes, everything is fine. Miss Gabler is attending one of the break-out sessions and I was wondering if you had a few minutes."

"Certainly, ma'am."

"Please sit."

Eric chooses the chair across from her. He looks like a good student holding a conference with his teacher. "You seem like such a nice young man," Julie says, using the words she rehearsed all morning. "I'd like to know more about you."

"Okay, what would you like to know?"

"Did you grow up in New Hampshire?"

"No. My dad's family is from Maine. But I grew up with my mom's family in Milwaukee."

"Milwaukee?"

"Yeah, my grandparents are still there. My mom died when I was five. They raised me."

"What about your father?"

"He disappeared when I was a baby. Maybe you've heard of him, his family was supposed to be pretty important. His name was Alexander Mundy."

Julie catches her breath. Eric can't help but notice. "You have heard of him, haven't you? What do you know about him, about his family? I've Googled and read some old newspapers but even my grandparents couldn't tell me much."

"I . . . I only know a little. Alexander's father was named George and most of the family died in a plane crash about twenty years ago."

"That much I know. My father disappeared a couple of months later."

"Is that why you took this job, to be in New England and learn more about your family?"

"Partially, but the Mount Washington is itself too good a career opportunity to pass up."

She wants to ask him more and he wants to tell her more, but a buzzing interrupts them. Its Eric's pager; he's wanted in a staff meeting. "Please, Mrs. Halloran, can we talk about this later?"

Julie agrees, wondering just where their next conversation will lead.

****

"Mrs. St. John, I'm sure you'll love what we can show you."

There are many things Karen misses about living in New York. She misses her penthouse and her charity events; she misses the museums and the shows; she misses the vibrancy of city life. She even misses her friends, such as they are. But what Karen misses most is the shopping. When first arriving years ago, she was limited to discount stores like Century 21 and the funky little shops of the East Village. Those days are long gone. Now Karen shops in the rarified world of Fifth Avenue. Places like Chanel and Dior and Tiffany all became second homes to her.

At this moment, she sits comfortably in the couture department on the fourth floor of Bergdorf-Goodman where a personal shopper readies some clothes by Marchesa. Karen likes the designs the two British women create; they are simple and elegant and flattering to her figure. Bergdorf's is one of the few places in America when you buy their wares.

While waiting, Karen pulls out her cell phone and texts Denise. Funeral or no funeral, she will need her assistant immediately. There is too much business to conduct (and too much shopping).

Models begin strutting before her in frocks most people can't afford. Karen plans stay in this beautiful Beaux-Arts department store the entire day. She will lunch in the restaurant on the seventh floor, and then she'll luxuriate downstairs on the Beauty Level with facials and other special treatments.

"I always love what I see here."

****

Everyone is quiet on the drive to the Radisson. Chloe suggested it since Jack, Joe and their son spent so much time there. Besides, Mrs. Bologna has a suite upstairs and wants to spend some quality time with her grandson.

The Radisson has set aside a meeting room for them, and the hotel's atrium restaurant, the Café on the Park, is providing a buffet of light dishes. Everyone remains quiet, very quiet. It's an awkward silence, the kind that happens only when people are unsure what they can safely talk about.

Denise motions to Jack. He steps over to her and she whispers the problem: Mrs. St. John wants her to fly to New York tonight. They could return at any time. The best chance he gets to search her house without getting caught is this evening. "I can give you a spare key and the security password."

"Shit, I can't; not tonight. I just buried Joe and Greg wants us to spend some time together while Little Jack is upstairs with his grandma."

"It's got to be tonight, Jack."

He takes a moment to think. *Who can I trust?* Jack immediately rules out Aaron and Chloe; a cop isn't likely to go sneaking into someone's house. Nick also flies back to New York tonight. That leaves one person. So, while they are alone at the buffet, Jack briefly explains the situation to Patrick.

"What the hell am I supposed to be looking for?"

"I don't know dude; that's the point. Who knows what else she's hiding. You care about Greg and Julie, right? Well, I love Greg. This secret could hurt them, and I bet it's just the tip. You don't go from being a small town college professor's daughter to becoming Mrs. Martin St. John by being a good girl."

Patrick frowns. "Fine."

✳✳✳✳

"Dear, secrets like this have a way of getting out. I warned your mother about that months ago."

Julie is wheeling Agnes through the hotel's Great Hall toward the Dartmouth Room, where one of the conference's beak-out sessions is about to begin.

"So, you think I should come right out and tell him the truth."

"Yes, but carefully, tactfully. Remember what a shock this has been for you. Imagine what it will be like for him."

✳✳✳✳

Jack has mixed feelings about turning his son over to Mrs. Bologna, even for a night. "Just remember: I'm his father and I have custody. Our marriage and Joe's will make that carved in stone."

It's late afternoon and the sober reception is winding down and everyone is going their separate ways. "You will see him in the morning," she assures him. Joe was worried about his stepfather's attempts to take their son. But with Vincent in custody, his mother insists that the boy will be returned safely.

"I just want to get to know him better and him me. I want to be able to visit him from time to time." A tear crawls down her cheek. "I've lost two husbands and now my daughter has been taken from me --- not once, but twice. I haven't the strength to do anything more."

Ann spent the remainder of the day in her room, crying. Gretchen tried to bring her lunch, then dinner, but Ann refused all food. As the day rolled on, the housekeeper made various attempts to rouse her. They failed.

Eventually, Ann has cried herself out. She is lying on the bed and staring at the ceiling. A sharp knock at the door startles her. "Please, Gretchen, I've told you before: I just want to be alone."

"I'm sorry Mrs. Davis," the muffled voice explains. "But the senator's office is on the phone. They say it's urgent." *Urgent? What could be so damned urgent?*

Ann reluctantly rises and opens the door. Gretchen hands her the cordless. On the other end is Richard's chief of staff: he's been arrested in Virginia on a DUI charge. It will hit the press by morning.

****

Agnes has gone to bed early. At 95, she simply hasn't the stamina. "They wanted me on this trip into town, but I'm just not as young as I used to be." But she insists on one thing: that Julie tells her brother the truth tonight. This is why she is sitting in The Cave, a former speakeasy on the hotel's lower level. It was here, behind stone walls and under a low ceiling, some of the Mt. Washington's more colorful guests used to while away their evenings.

Julie orders a lime Perrier; she needs to remain sober and in control.

Eric soon arrives fresh from ending his shift. A smile crosses his face when he sees her. The young man orders a Bacardi & Coke before sitting across from her. It suddenly occurs to Julie that he may think this is some kind of a date. It reminds her of her own thoughts just a day before. *Be careful, this can't become even more of a Greek tragedy.*

"So, Eric, how did your day go?"

"Fun but exhausting."

"You really love your job, huh?"

"Yeah, it's interesting. I meet the coolest people. This isn't just past history, its history every day."

Julie can't help but smile at his enthusiasm and wishes they had grown up together. *I wonder what that would have been like.*

"I really appreciate your talking to me earlier today."

"That's okay," he shrugs; "I'm an open book."

She wishes more people were. "You probably heard about my father, Senator King, passing away recently."

"It was on the news; I'm sorry, by the way. It must have been tough."

"Yes, it has been difficult. But shortly after he died, I learned something really surprising."

"What's that?"

"I'm adopted."

"Really? That _is_ big."

"The woman I have known all my life as Aunt Karen --- my mother's sister --- is the woman who gave birth to me."

"Wow; it sounds like a real-life soap opera." Eric suddenly catches himself and adds, "Sorry I shouldn't have said that."

"Don't worry. Being a Halloran is a little like being in a soap opera. Anyway, not long after that I discovered who my biological father is." Eric looks at her quizzically, so Julie comes right out with it: "Alexander Mundy."

Eric shakes his head. "No way."

"I'm afraid that it's true."

"Is that why you came to Bretton Woods, to find me and tell me this?"

"No, I really did come to help Agnes. Finding you was just a bizarre coincidence."

Eric rises, saying "this is too weird for me" and walks out.

✶✶✶✶

Little Jack is spending the night with his grandmother. Patrick has gone. Nick is back in New York. Denise went to pack for her flight. Aaron and Chloe are at home. This leaves Jack and Greg, relaxing not in Joe's apartment but in Jack's. It seems more appropriate to both men.

"Don't take it the wrong way, Greg, but I'm not in the mood for sex tonight." They are relaxing on the leather sofa, sipping a couple of beers.

"I figured that, but I did think you'd get a kick out of this," he holds up a DVD.

"What's that?"

"It's the recording Bradley used to blackmail me with."

"Have you seen it?"

"No, things have been too crazy. But I'm sure you'll have fun watching it."

"Wow, dude, you must really think I'm sick; to want to watch you do porno."

"Am I wrong?"

"Fuck, no, I need something. Put it in."

Greg turns on the TV and DVD player and slips the disc inside. Soon a menu pops up on the screen: one choice is labeled "Halloran Recording" and the other "Special Message." Jack picks up the remote and selects the first. A few seconds later and they see an image of a simple bedroom, with lots of used and cheap furniture. There are plants scattered about, mostly ferns. A bra and a pair of woman's jeans lay casually on a chair. A shower can be heard from the adjacent bathroom. Seeing all of this is like a weird trip in time for Greg who watches himself enter the room, strip to his briefs and toss his clothes on top of the bra.

"Dude," Jack chuckles, "your hard-on is so obvious!"

Greg smiles, more from embarrassment that anything else. On screen, a nude Mark emerges from the bathroom toweling himself off and saying "I was wondering how fast you'd show up."

Jack lets out a low whistle at the sight of Bradley's toned body. Greg remembers how hot that man was, and still is. "I didn't want to waste any time," video Greg answers. "They won't be gone forever."

He must have taped this on the night of Julie's shower. Back on the screen, Mark steps up to him and brushes a hand across Greg's bare chest. "When the wives are away, the husbands will play, huh?"

"Something like that. The usual amount?"

"Sure."

Mark --- and Jack --- smile at video Greg's tight rear as he bends over to retrieve cash from his wallet. The hustler takes his money and sets it on top of the dresser next to one of the many ferns in the room. He turns back to take the other man in his arms. "What's with all the damned greenery?" Greg asks as Mark's hands slide his briefs to the floor.

"The wife thinks the place is ugly, so she bought all kinds of shit like plants." Mark leans in to give Greg a slow, sexy kiss. "We've got at least a couple of hours this time, dude, so why not take things slow and get your money's worth?" Greg kisses him again, pressing their chests together. They fall to the bed and the picture changes to another angle. *Oh fuck, he had more than one camera and actually edited the thing together!* The two men are showed making out with Greg caressing Mark's broad chest and biceps. Mark begins licking his client all over, from lips to nipples to stomach. He takes Greg into his mouth to get him all slick, hard and ready. Then Mark straddles his client, sitting down on him, taking him deep inside. Video Greg moans, "Damn your ass is great. I love being inside you."

"Better than your wife's pussy?"

Greg flinches as he watches the video. "Do you want me to turn it off?" Jack asks him. Greg shakes his head. *I may as well face this.*

Back on the screen, Mark begins to slide himself up and down, slowly at first, then a little faster and then even more until Greg's back arches and eyes close. *So that's what I look like when I cum.* Mark starts to pull him out when Greg stops him. "Don't you want to cum? I can suck you or jerk you off."

"Can't dude, got to save it for the misses. She expects me when she comes back from partying with your wife." Mark rolls himself off Greg to lie next to him. "So, can I count on you after the wedding? You're my favorite client, you know."

"Sure," Video Greg smiles. "Julie hasn't had much interest in sex since the pregnancy."

"And every guy's gotta get off. Congrats, by the way. I didn't get a chance to tell you earlier."

"Thanks; so, what's it like married to the farm girl?"

Mark shrugs. "It's okay. She can be a real pain sometimes. I think she's convinced that she can do better."

"What, better than you?"

"Better than me, better than her old man, better than this whole fucking town."

"I don't envy you, dude. I haven't spent much time with her but she really gets on my nerves. I have to put up with her for Julie's sake, but I can't really stand her otherwise." Video Greg looks at the clock on the nightstand. "Well, I should get going." He gets out of bed and starts to dress.

"Why so soon?"

"Sorry, but Ben and my old man want to have drinks while the girls have their little party."

"Too bad." Mark watches Greg get dressed. "Be sure to call me after the honeymoon."

Greg smiles back and says with a wink, "count on it," and leaves the house. Mark rises and returns to the bathroom and the screen goes black, then the menu reappears.

"What an ass."

"Yeah, but a hot looking ass."

"Not him, me. I was about to marry a woman I really loved and still, still I was fucking around on the side."

"I'm not sure hookers count."

"That's what I used to think. Not any more."

Jack selects the menu's second option, "Special Message". A different room appears: a cheap nondescript motel room, like the kind found on so many highways. Mark is sitting on the bed, dressed in just a towel, and smiling. "Well, Greggy, I hope you like our little porno. I got to tell you, I seriously thought about destroying all the copies after you pay me. But then, I got to thinking: that would be stupid. This video is the best investment I've ever made. But don't worry; I won't release it, as long as I know I can count on you when I need you. Later, dude." The screen goes dark again.

After a brief and tense moment, Greg mutters angrily, "that fucking bastard."

****

Mark is nearly ready. His trick tonight is a wealthy older woman who insists that her gentlemen dress appropriately. So he takes another shower and slips into the expensive Prada suit she bought for him. Mark finds the whole thing silly; after all, he'll be stripping shortly after arriving at her Park Avenue apartment. Still, this is part of what the lady pays for.

At least tonight it <u>is</u> a lady. Mark gets tired of the gray haired men who normally hire him. They are old and flabby and sometimes he has trouble getting hard.

Someone knocks on his door; it is an elegant, dignified yet strongly determined knock. *Who the hell could that be?* No one buzzed from outside the building, so it must be a neighbor. Mark peers through the peephole. *Oh, shit, not her!*

"Mark, darling, I know that you are there," Karen St. John says. "Please open up."

"You've paid me, so get lost!"

"Lover, you know me better than that."

With a grumble, he opens the door.

Karen enters his apartment, striding in her lady like manner, and looks about her. "So, this is life in Greenwich Village." She observes the exposed brick walls, big windows and expensive leather furniture. "It's not my taste, but it does seem to suit you."

"You can't stay."

"I know lover; you have a client tonight."

"How do you know that?"

"Because I'm the one who recommended you --- didn't she tell you? Catherine Rutherford is a dear old friend of mine. Sadly, her husband just doesn't please her anymore. Between you and me, I think he's impotent."

When will I ever get this crazy bitch out of my life?

"Now, that suit you are wearing --- Prada, isn't it --- that <u>must</u> be Catherine's doing. She always had excellent taste."

"Why are you here, Karen?"

She steps over to <u>him</u> and caresses his rugged cheek with her soft, manicured hand. "I'm just reminding you how important I am --- and how I usually get my way." With that, she kisses him and strolls out the door.

✲✲✲✲

Patrick steps up to the door. He has never been to Karen St. John's house before. But he likes what he sees: a beautiful old Victorian, with lots of windows and a wrap-around porch. He can just imagine, decades ago, well dress ladies sitting here, sipping their morning tea, while watching the men walk to work at the Halloran textile mill.

He opens the door, keys in the security code, and turns on a light. The foyer is small, but attractive. It has the look of a place recently, and expensively, decorated. Patrick imagines that the entire house is like this, but is surprised when he walks into the living room: it's empty. There is no furniture at all, just a rug on the polished, hard wood floor. *That's weird.* Glancing around he can see the dining room fully furnished. In fact, a brief stroll reveals that the only part of the house that is empty is the living room. *That is _really_ weird.*

Patrick isn't sure what he's looking for. He starts in Karen's little study. The desk is exquisite, obviously an antique, although he doesn't know enough to identify its style. The draws are filled with financial statements and memos involving the St. John Group. *Shit, she's richer than I thought.* He also finds a copy of the agreement selling Karen shares in Halloran Enterprises. It's all very interesting, but not incriminating. *What the hell do they expect me to find?*

Denise mentioned that Karen keeps the adoption papers in her closet. So Patrick mounts the stairs to the second floor. The meticulous master bedroom is impressive, with a handsome, old four-poster bed dominating the space. Patrick opens the closet door. It is filled with designer clothes worth thousands of dollars. On the shelf above are some shoes, a file box and a thick envelope. He finds the birth certificate and adoption papers inside the envelope. *So, it's true! Who the fuck could imagine it?* He returns the documents and envelope to their place and pulls out the file box. It's heavy, very heavy. Patrick plops it onto the bed. *This is a waste of time. She's probably got tax forms or some such shit in here.*

Then he opens the box. Inside, carefully organized, are a series of folders. Each has a person's name on the tab. He recognizes most of them: Lewis Halloran, Lilly Halloran, Greg Halloran . . . *What the fuck?*

Pulling out the Lewis file, he begins to read. And what he reads scares him as nothing else ever has.

The Original Faraway Hill

When author James A. Richards began writing the *Faraway Hill* trilogy, he could not find any information to confirm where the fictional town of the TV series was located. Since many soaps (especially early soaps) were set in either New England or the Midwest, he selected the former. There was also very little information available about characters and plots.

After the trilogy was first published, Richards was contacted by broadcast industry veteran Clarke Ingram, whose thirty year career in radio had him work both on-air and in management. Since retirement, Ingram has become something of an Early TV expert who collects material related to the DuMont Network (1946-1956). He also manages a web site at www.dumontnetwork.com.

FARAWAY HILL

E. Cattle, Photo

By JENA PHELPS

"Faraway Hill" represents television's first long-range attempt to bring radio's "soap opera" to television. It has completed its initial series of ten episodes over WABD and, according to David P. Lewis, director of the program for Caples Agency, the second series is now being prepared for early airing.

Lewis' visual interpretation of the radio program may not meet with the approval of some critics of the established media of film, stage, and radio. But **Telescreen's** canvas of televiewers indicates their approval—and they, when all is said and done, are the final judge. In conducting this canvas, it was interesting to note that the farther away from New York the program was received, the more appropriate and real the farm setting of the story seemed to be.

From the standpoint of program form, it is **Telescreen's** view that the daily dramatic serial of radio is actually more favorable to video than to radio. With radio, in conveying emotion "a kind of luridness is inevitable," to quote Raphael Hayes, radio writer (**Telescreen**, Fall, 1946) because "it is the spoken word that must underscore action." It would not surprise us if the "soap opera" serial, the subject of more criticism than any other radio program on the air today, will become one of the least criticised programs on television.

The dramatic serial can be handled more subtly when telecast. Intensely subjective, it is concerned primarily with motivation and emotion between a **few** characters rather than with action, plot or "cast of a hundred." Television also permits a swifter, more facile development of the story. And intimacy, one of television's most prized characteristics, is exploited in this type of drama, lending itself as it does to the closeup technique of story-telling.

In Lewis' video form of the serial, the dialogue of the radio form is retained, making it possible for a home viewer-listener to follow the story while out of range of the telescreen.

Because the emphasis is placed on people and emotions, less rehearsing and fewer and simpler sets are required. Production costs are actually lower than in some other video forms.

From the talent standpoint, memorizing scripts has not proven to be the bugaboo anticipated, according to Lewis. Cast members can memorize and rehearse the requirements of three quarter-hour programs weekly. The problem in television is that lines cannot be read from script as they are in radio. Lewis admits that because of this fact, the radio practice of starring an actor or actress in various shows running concurrently, cannot be done in television; and, moreover, that this may have a bearing on the cost of the video dramatic serial. Actually, this may prove to be an advantage, Lewis believes, resulting in better entertainment worth more of the sponsor's money.

The widespread use of this dramatic serial form for television

1. (Upper right) In "Faraway Hill", Karen St. John (Flora Campbell) stands on the summit after which the farm is named and surveys the homestead of her cousin whom she has come to visit. 2. (Lower left) Shortly after her arrival at Faraway Hill, Karen is introduced to Charlie White (Mel Brandt), her cousin's foster son. He warns her that life on the farm is quite different from the city. 3. Learning that Faraway Hill is the homestead of plain "dirt farmers", instead of the luxurious country estate she had expected, Karen is impelled to leave immediately, except that

Ingram emailed Richards some of the items he has discovered about the "Faraway Hill" television series, part of which is published on these pages.

An article written by Jena Phelps for *Telescreen* magazine reports that "Faraway Hill" is set in a farm town in Middle America. The series starred Flora Campbell (1911-1978) as Karen St. John, the wealthy widow who visits her rural cousins where she begins a forbidden romance with a farmhand played by Mel Brandt (1919-2008). The series aired live from DuMont's studio inside New York City's iconic Wanamaker Department Store.

A Unique Twist to The Tele Soap Opera Given By Caples' Man Lewis →

A specter that has been tormenting television—lurking always in the background—is the threatening visual counterpart of radio's soap opera. Will television be beset by the moronic daytime serial?

Some stations and agencies, particularly Ruthrauff & Ryan, have tried their hand at adapting radio daytime serials on television and even gone so far as to write original material. The results were not particularly encouraging to agency men searching for a visual formula for the tried-and-true housewife-audience thriller.

It now appears that the video serial drama is a reality; for quietly down at the John Wanamaker-DuMont studio, a successful, stream-of-consciousness formula is being evolved, judging by the opening episodes of *Faraway Hill*. The man responsible is David P. Lewis, television director of the Caples ad agency, who has been experimenting in television, trying various types of shows—gag varieties, dramas, interviews, and now the serial—since April of this year.

Caples' Tele Policy

The Caples Company, primarily known as a travel agency, serving railroad and resort clients (Union Pacific Railroad, American Express, Railroad Express) who have not thought of radio as a good advertising medium, believes that television is a powerful visual advertising medium for its clients. Consequently, the agency set aside a budget and definitely decided to experiment with television to acquaint itself with television techniques and program formats so that it will be ready to serve its clients with commercial television. Caples firmly believes that there eventually will be television broadcasting eighteen hours a day—and that not too far off.

In experimenting with television, the agency specifically wants to find out:

(1) What kind of formats will be good television.

(2) How to produce them on television.

The man selected for the job, dark, ministerial-appearing David P. Lewis, had never been in a television control room up to eight months ago, never written for television although he had ten years in advertising, mostly in Chicago; and, prior to that, worked in summer stock. He joined the Caples Agency three years ago to handle its Union Pacific radio show, and came to New York in January, 1946.

Lewis had to learn television pretty much on his own, doing all his own writing as well as production. The first tele-show he put on, *The Red Benson Show*, a gag variety, was on April 25th, and since then he has written, directed and produced twenty-three shows up to the middle of October when *Faraway Hill* started. The serial is based on an unfinished novel Lewis wrote years ago.

Stream-of-Consciousness

In developing the video serial format, which utilizes an "all-seeing voice," Lewis was hunting for a manner of presentation which would not require 100 per cent viewer attention, which would allow the housewife to turn away and go on peeling potatoes or knitting and at the same time follow the program, with story action cued by a voice line. Further he wanted a means of probing into the heroine, analyzing her reactions so that the audience could see her objectively and sympathetically. This he accomplished by the "stream-of-consciousness" voice, an example of which follows:

MEDIUM TWO-SHOT	LOUISE: Dad didn't mention it when he wrote because he said you had your own dead to bury; and besides, he was afraid you might not come if you knew how Mother was and he wanted you to come.
	KAREN: I almost feel . . .
	LOUISE: Oh, please don't feel that way, we really wanted you. I just wanted to warn you about Mother. She's all right, only the war and Buddy are two things we never mention at Faraway Hill!
FILM SEQUENCE	MUSIC: (Interlude, fading to Voice)
	THE VOICE: Turn back, turn back, Karen St. John! Something inside you is sounding a warning. This is no place for you! What you are seeking is surcease of trouble, not sharing the wearisome burdens of others. Where is the country estate you were dreaming of? How can you stay! You must leave in the morning . . . you cannot stay a summer!
Dissolve to CLOSEUP OF SIGN AT ENTRANCE OF HOMESTEAD.	
	MUSIC: (Up Full)

Mr. Lewis considers *Faraway Hill* a shade better than the radio soap opera.

(See review "Faraway Hill," page 29)

ROMANCE . . .

"Do you know what it is to be madly in love, with someone who loves you?"—from "Faraway Hill."

According to the Internet Movie Database (IMDB), Flora Campbell continued to appear on various television programs until the late 1960s as well as in the acclaimed 1966 film adaptation of the controversial novel *The Group* (she played Jessica Walter's mother). Mel Brandt shifted his professional focus from acting to announcing, including for the daytime soap opera "The Doctors" and, briefly in 1982, for "Saturday Night Live."

STATION WABD

WABD began as an experimental station launched in 1938 by television manufacturer Allen B. Dumont (1901-1965) with the call letters W2XVT. The station received a commercial license in 1944 which is when it became WABD (using DuMont's initials) and located on VHF channel 4. In 1945 it was moved to channel 5.

The station became the flagship of the DuMont Television Network, often broadcasting from a studio built inside the Wanamaker Department Store at 770 Broadway.

Today, the station uses the call letters WNYW and is the flagship station for the Fox Broadcasting Company. A detailed history of WABD/WNYW is available on Wikipedia. The Wanamaker store is now an office building where major companies like the Huffington Post and Facebook are among the tenants.

EPISODE SIX

"There are times," Patrick Halloran's father once told him, "when you just man up and do what needs to be done."

This needs to be done. It's nearly Midnight and Patrick has arrived at the empty Millyard. The warm, still night air gives the complex a very different aura, something like a medieval fortress that has been abandoned for centuries. The mood seems fitting to Patrick, considering the macabre task ahead of him.

Inside the Halloran offices, he powers up the Ricoh copier. Carefully, he duplicates each sheet of paper in each file before returning it to its precise place in the box. He can't help but read them. Each file contains what can only be called a project plan: the type of logical, methodical plan that anyone in a business class learns to draft. But these aren't plans for a store or a restaurant. These are one woman's plans for committing murder.

Patrick shudders at Karen St. John's cold, detached and detailed work. One describes how she murdered Martin St. John's first wife, then Martin himself. Another details how Karen killed Aunt Lilly. In each case, she makes certain their deaths look like something else. Uncle Lewis' murder is different. Karen wanted to confront him. So she pulled the trigger herself and framed Munroe Gale.

There are times when Patrick has to stop, and sit, and gather himself. Reading these papers make him sick.

Karen has tried to kill Greg, not once but twice. The first was poisoning his tea. The second was the fire at King's Korner, which was meant to remove Ben King and Mark Bradley as well. Each failed and, in a logical and professional manner, the files include reasons why they failed including a "lessons learned" section.

What astounds him most of all is that she would keep these things. It makes no sense to him, until he arrives at the last folder. In it, she has laid out different plans --- to write her memoir and having it published posthumously. *This woman is a psychopath.*

The last of the copies are made. He puts them and the originals in the truck of the car. He drives back to Faraway Hill and returns Karen's box to her closet. As he does this, Patrick can't help but think of his father and his father's advice. There are times when a man must do something on his own. There are also times when a man needs his Brothers.

***

The sharp sound of stilettos on parquet jolts Denise awake. It takes her a moment to gain her bearings until she remembers that she spent the night at Karen St. John's penthouse. *What the hell is going on?* Denise slips out of bed clad only in an extra large T-shirt and undies. Looking around she spies her suitcase on the floor, bends over and pulls out her satin robe. All the while she nervously wonders what her strange boss is up to this time.

Emerging from the guest room, she finds Mrs. St. John and another woman --- a slim, middle-aged woman wearing an expensive dress and stilettos and carrying a clipboard --- striding down the short hall. Denise follows them into the living room. Mrs. St John smiles at her. "Good morning dear, I trust you slept well."

"Yes, ma'am, thank you."

"This is my realtor, Mrs. Miller."

Mrs. Miller's smile carves the wrinkles that numerous plastic surgeries have failed to completely erase. "Good morning."

"Denise is my personal assistant. She flew in late last night and the poor dear needed the extra sleep." She also needed a <u>place </u>to sleep; Denise had sublet her Manhattan apartment months ago.

The realtor steps to the window and its magnificent view of Central Park. "This is prime property, Mrs. St. John. I have no doubt that we can get you top dollar and fast." *She's selling? I can't believe it.* Denise turns to her boss but before she can ask anything, the lady instructs her to shower and change. "I have a whole list of errands for you to run. As soon as my business is over, we'll be heading back to Faraway Hill --- permanently."

✳✳✳✳

"We'll be heading back to Faraway Hill tomorrow," Agnes says cautiously examining Julie. "You may want to talk to Eric again."

They are having breakfast in the hotel's main dining room, a magnificent space with a high ceiling bordered by beautiful Tiffany windows and featuring exquisite chandeliers.

"I know," Julie answers after sipping her coffee. "But I don't think that he wants to speak to me again. He was pretty upset."

"What did he say?"

"He doesn't believe me. Oh, he wasn't rude about it or anything, but he doesn't believe that Alexander Mundy is my father."

"Or maybe he was too shocked to fully accept it."

"Maybe," Julie replies as she spots Eric at the dining room's entry. A folded newspaper is tucked under his armpit. He looks uncomfortable and hesitant. It takes him a moment to screw up the courage to step over to their table. "I came to apologize, Mrs. Halloran."

"You have nothing to apologize for."

"Maybe, but . . . after talking to my grandmother last night I've come to realize that it's probably true, that we have the same dad."

Julie reaches out for his hand and gives it a supportive, sisterly squeeze. He smiles at her before remembering "I thought you should see this." He hands her this morning's copy of *USA Today*. "It's about your brother-in-law."

A big headline below the fold announces that Senator Richard Davis has been charged with driving under the influence.

****

Richard's Washington condo is fairly modest; just one bedroom and a small living/dining room. With home in Concord a short flight away, he has never had the need for more while in the nation's capital.

Ann is in the galley kitchen getting him a tall glass of ice water.

"What is that for?" Richard asks, sitting on the sofa nursing his aching and woozy head.

"Alcohol dehydrates you. This will help with your hangover."

"I wasn't aware you know so much about this."

"I grew up with an alcoholic, remember?"

He nods. He remembers. Ann arrived early this morning to find that he had already been released on bail and dozing fully clothed on the bed. This is a first offence and no one was hurt, so legally he has little to worry about. The political fallout may be different. "I suppose it's all over the news."

She hands him the glass. "You are on the cover of everything from the *Concord Monitor* to *USA Today*." He takes a sip and finds it surprisingly refreshing. "By the way, my mother called earlier and so did your daughter. Rebecca is really worried about you."

"I'll call her in a little while."

Ann sits next to him. "You were drinking because of me, weren't you?"

"No," he lies and not very well. *Aren't politicians supposed to be excellent liars?* "I just lost track of how much I drank."

"I know that, in me, you got more than you bargained for."

"Ann ---"

"But I do love you, and I want to make this work."

He simply nods and takes another drink of water.

****

Patrick dials the number. It's a number that never appears on a caller ID or in a phone book. It's a number few people have.

The light of a new day and hundreds of people bring life back to the Millyard. This includes Patrick, who is nervously sitting alone in his newly assigned office at Halloran Enterprises. He is still groggy from getting so little sleep.

Three rings and the call is answered.

"Salutem," a rich, baritone voice says in Latin. This is the Brothers' major domo. That is all he is known by, at least by most of the Brothers. The major domo manages the lodge and acts as a conduit to the Elders. And, like so much else with the Brothers, the formalities of ritual must be observed.

"Salutem honestum domine," Patrick greets him. "Hoc est Frater Patrick Halloran."

"Salutem Frater Patrick."

"Ego formaliter petentibus faciem Seniorum." This is the ritual request of a Brother to schedule a meeting with the Elders. The major domo responds by asking, again in Latin, what's the purpose of the meeting Patrick is requesting. He explains it is involving a crime against a Brother by saying "me acelus Fratris renuntiare."

The major domo tells him that the arrangements will be made. "Bene faciamus spectent."

"Gratias, honestum domine," Patrick thanks him and hangs up.

****

Greg's first meeting of the day isn't for another hour. So, he sits in his office, sipping hot coffee and gazing out the big window at the century old brick buildings. Greg noticed how exhausted Patrick was on their drive in this morning. He yawned twice but insisted he is okay. Still, Greg wonders what he was doing all night. *Did he have a date?* Greg certainly remembers being tired after a long night --- and a long fuck --- while tomcatting around NYU. But it doesn't seem to him that Patrick has spent enough time in Faraway Hill to hook-up with anyone.

Of course, it didn't take Greg much time finding hook-ups when he first returned to town. The thought of sex reminds him of Mark Bradley and the asshole's blackmail. Greg has tried reaching him several times since seeing the video, but all he gets is voicemail.

Turning the chair around, Greg sets the cup aside and opens the folder he brought into work today. He found it just after Ben's death in his father's study. On it is written in Lewis' hand, "Greg & the Brothers". Greg opens it to reread lined yellow sheets with references to "The Brothers of Thebes". These include comments by his dad such as "ask about initiation process for older plebes" and "get Robert to help lobby the elders."

As he had done before, Greg logs on to his computer and again Googles "The Brothers of Thebes". The Wikipedia entry he read earlier is the first on the list of results. He clicks the link to read it once more: an "alleged secret society of influential men . . . very active behind the scenes of American politics and economy" that is inspired by "a troop of elite citizen soldiers consisting of 150 to 300 male couples drawn from the ancient Greek city of Thebes . . . Who encouraged the men to be sexually intimate as a means of cementing their loyalty to the corps."

Is this really what Dad's referring to? ". . . The Brothers were formed in the late 1700s by a group of American men." *That would fit the history of the Hallorans.* "Most of these men were 'gatekeepers', those who worked as secretaries and aides-de-camp for many of the new country's leaders." *That describes John Halloran.*

Two pieces of information he finds very interesting: one about how "only the sons, grandsons and nephews of existing or past Brothers are allowed to apply for consideration" and another referring to "a heavy emphasis on sexual experiences" among the members.

Greg stares at the screen. *Could this be real? It sounds too fantastical, like something the* National Inquirer *would publish.* There seems to be one possible way to find the answer. It lies in Lewis' comment about "get Robert to help lobby the elders." Greg opens up Outlook and sends his cousin a short email asking when they can speak. He doesn't say what about, mostly because he isn't sure how to ask.

But he's going to ask the question, one way or another.

****

It took awhile, but Matthew finally found him.

Billy wasn't in his room or the library. He'd finished kitchen duty early and no one knew where he went. Matthew checked out nearly every part of the lodge that plebes have access. Eventually, through a window, he saw Billy outside on the back patio.

"Hey, dude," Billy greets him with a glance. He is perched on the stone fence, reading. It's the Brothers' rulebook. Matthew has found it dense and filled with outdated language. That shouldn't be surprising since most of it was written 150 years ago. Only the supplements are recent and two of them deal with the same things: AIDS. One, issued in the early 1980s, offered modified rules to the sexual rituals. But with the pandemic's peak in the past, another supplement essentially restored the old rites.

They share the same tutor, and Justin has been advising Matthew that he needs to bond more with the other plebes. "These guys are going to be more than friends to you." Justin explained. "These are dudes that you will know for the rest of your life, dudes you'll need to trust." So Matthew studies the other young man. Billy is wearing denim shorts and a simple T-shirt, which clings tightly to his torso. Matthew can see his lean physique and well defined muscles.

"You like what you see?"

"Sorry," Matthew blushes. Billy slams the book shut and smiles. "It's okay. Justin tells me you having some problems getting with some of the guys."

"Yeah, and he says you can help."

"Sure; a couple of guys are meeting in my room tonight. After dinner. You can come, too."

"I can?"

"Yep, just don't wear much --- like, just your robe --- got it?"

He gets it.

****

Mrs. Bologna kept her promise. A smiling Little Jack returned home after spending a comforting night with his grandmother. Jack is so relieved that he finds it much easier to be civil to her than it was at the funeral. The drive to Manchester International Airport is almost pleasant.

They arrive in time to check her luggage and spend a few relaxing moments in the VIP lounge. Every time Jack comes here, his mind returns to the day when he and the Hallorans gathered here to meet Greg and Julie. That, too, had to do with a loss.

"Grandma, will you come and visit again?"

"Of course, darling; whenever you want."

In the middle of this exchange, Jack gets a long-awaited text from Patrick Halloran. In it he says he found nothing at St. John's house. *Maybe that's it, maybe that's the woman's only secret.* If so, then there may still be hope for him and Greg.

Father and son escort the grandmother to the TSA check-in. Jack is surprised when he gets a hug, too. Once she disappears from view, Jack takes the boy's hand. "Why does Grandma always call Papa her daughter?"

Damn, I knew she'd confuse him. "Did she say that last night?"

Little Jack nods. "I don't get it."

"Maybe, it's just her way." It's the only explanation Jack can think of. His son is still confused but says nothing more about it.

****

Richard spends the day dealing with the fallout of his arrest. He is either on the phone with staff or in bed recovering from his hangover.

Ann, on the other had, spends the day watching TV. She doesn't dare go outside where reporters are sure to ask her questions she'd prefer not to answer. By mid-afternoon she has grown sick of repeats and game shows. The news channels' top stories include "the senator from New Hampshire arrested last night" on a DUI charge. They repeat this often.

She can hear the phone ring again. This time she can hear through the bedroom door a muffled "come on up." *Who can it be?*

A moment later and someone knocks on the condo's front door. Ann opens it. Standing there, smiling is a handsome man in his 50s wearing an expensive suit and surrounded by two attractive young men about her age. "Yes?"

"You must be Ann."

"I am," she answers, confused. "Who are you?"

"Sorry; I'm Judge Edgar Massie and these are two of my aides. Richard is expecting me."

Ann invites them inside, still confused about why these men are here. She walks over to the bedroom door. "Sweetheart, Judge Massie is here." The door opens and Richard, looking sober and refreshed in clean clothes, emerges. "Good. The timing is perfect."

"Perfect for what?"

"For getting married."

He still love me is the thought that first crosses her mind. At least, until he adds "announcing your pregnancy will change the story. The scandal of last night will be put to rest."

"Of course," Ann fights back tears. This is just about saving his career. "You're right."

Within minutes their marriage finally becomes legal with Judge Massie declaring "I now pronounce you husband and wife." There is a kiss, but it lacks the passion she has come to know from him.

But, at least now, she is truly Mrs. Davis.

✱✱✱✱

Mark Bradley strips off every piece of clothing the moment he returns home. He prefers to be nude; it's more comfortable for him. Especially after spending the morning giving head to not one but three clients --- all old men who wanted the thrill of being blown in their fancy executive offices. Mark actually spent more time on the subway than on his knees: going from the Village to Madison Avenue to Wall Street to Times Square and, finally, back in the Village.

Throwing his clothes in a pile, he steps in the shower and lets the hot water blast away a dirty, but profitable, morning. Mark hasn't any clients scheduled for two days, and the next one is a woman. He can relax in the meantime.

Mark steps out of the shower and towels off. He can hear the cell ring in the other room. *It's him again,* he chuckles. *The dude just won't give up.* Mark grabs another towel, a dry one and plops naked on the leather sofa. He answers the phone with a hearty "Hey Greggy."

"Where the fuck have you been? I've been trying to reach you all day."

"Sorry, dude, but your not my only customer."

"I want the master to that video."

"No can do, Greggy. I might it need it some day."

"You little prick --- " Mark cuts him off, leans back, and laughs.

✱✱✱✱

In all the years that Denise Sullivan lived in the city, there were certain places she longed to go. Places that are quintessentially New York. But she seldom had the money to do it. Finally, she knows someone who does. *Too bad,* Denise thinks, *that she's a crazy bitch.*

They have come to 21, the famous former speakeasy on West 52nd Street. The two women strode beneath the painted cast iron lawn jockeys and were greeted by a charming young man wearing a suit and sporting a baseball cap with "21" printed on it. "Welcome back, Mrs. St. John. We've missed you."

"And I've missed all of you, Aaron."

Everything about the restaurant amazes Denise. Dangling from the black ceiling are toys --- toy cars, toy planes, toy boats --- thousands of them, all donated by celebrities. Seated at the tables, enjoying their meals on red and white checkered cloths, are people she has seen before; but never in person. In one corner is an Academy Award winning actress, dining with what appear to be old friends. A well-known comedian and his wife are just steps away. The mayor is entertaining guests at the far side of the room.

Several of them glance up to smile at Mrs. St. John. A few of the men smile at Denise, too, but this seems mostly about her tight black dress.

They are escorted up to the second floor. This dining room is just as amazing as the one below, but in a very different way. While the main space is dark and private, this one is small and bright. Along the walls are vivid murals of New York City, depicting scenes that Denise guesses to be from the 20s or the 30s. Beneath them is a beautiful gold upholstered seat running the entire length.

Here, too. Denise sees famous people eating and laughing.

She and Mrs. St. John are brought to a little square table with a pristine white cloth. The menu is heavy on seafood but Denise is craving something more basic. Mrs. St. John orders the sautéed halibut and Denise the filet mignon. At her boss's suggestion, they both order the Chilled Senegalese Soup as an appetizer. "It's scrumptious," she tells Denise.

After ordering, Mrs. St. John asks her to review the day's errands. They all involved picking up things or dropping off things while the grand dame stayed in her posh penthouse. Denise knows that this is her job, but can't help but wonder if the lady is using her to be more efficient or to feel more regal. This is one of many questions she has, especially since Patrick Halloran texted her this afternoon. He found nothing suspicious in the house. Denise doesn't buy it, but hasn't had time to call Patrick.

The waiter brings them the soup. Denise finds it creamy and spicy, with chicken and green apples. It takes her a moment to realize that the spice is curry, and that Mrs. St. John is right in calling it "scrumptious".

"Mrs. St. John?"

"Yes, dear."

"Is it true," she asks carefully, diplomatically, "that you plan to leave New York forever?"

"Oh, we'll come and visit of course. But my family needs me." *Does that family include the daughter you gave up? What does this mean for the rest of us? What does this mean for me?* Denise realizes that she telegraphing when Mrs. St. John adds "don't worry, soon Faraway Hill will feel like home to you."

****

Jack and his son eat dinner in silence. They are in Joe's apartment having mac & cheese, one of the few things Jack knows how to cook. He considered going out somewhere or having something delivered, but it seems to him that they need some family time.

Unfortunately, this reminds him of his own family time: quiet dinners with his father grimacing every time one of his sons ventures a comment or an opinion.

Jack doesn't want to repeat the cycle with his son. "So, what should we do tomorrow?"

The boy silently shrugs.

"We can go to the SEE Science Center. You like that."

He shrugs again.

Jack worries and wonders what the boy must be thinking. He wishes he had someone to ask, someone to offer advice. For now, father and son eat in silence.

****

Ann and Richard eat their dinner in silence. This is their wedding night, but there is nothing romantic about it. Just some Chinese delivered to the condo, so that they don't have to be seen publicly. They have spent the entire awkward day within these four walls.

"We'll fly back to New Hampshire tomorrow," Richard explains between bites, "and tell your mother about the pregnancy then announce it at a press conference in Concord the day after."

"Sounds like a good plan," Ann nods. This is the last thing either of them says during the meal. Dinner ends as it began, in silence.

****

Matthew fidgets a little as he puts on the robe his mother gave him at Christmas. Despite what Billy told him, Matthew isn't completely naked underneath: he's also wearing a pair of clean, white briefs.

His bedroom is one of many, near the middle of a long hall on the second floor. This is where plebes stay. Upstairs are suites for the Brothers. Matthew steps out of his room and begins a slow walk, feeling a little like a condemned man approaching the gallows.

Matthew has done a few things with the other plebes, mostly masturbatory. It was finally Justin and some spiked tea that shattered his reticence. *This should be easy,* he tells himself, but isn't convinced.

Like the rest of the lodge, the hall radiates an aura of history and permanence and tradition. The hardwood floors are covered with antique Persian rugs. Pressed against the richly paneled walls are pieces of heavy oak furniture that must be a century old. Hung from these same walls are elegant oil paintings depicting landscapes from across New England. There is even one of the Halloran mansion, dating to the 1870s.

Most of the plebes' doors are closed. This is because many of the rooms are empty. But it's also because some plebes are bonding the way Matthew is supposed to. Passing one door, he can hear muffled voices. Curious, he presses an ear to the wood. Matthew listens to three, no four, guys saying things like "take it easier, dude" and "man, I'm gonna cum soon."

Some are bonding in more conventional ways. As he resumes his walk, Matthew passes an open door where, inside, a couple of plebes are blasting away bad guys with an X-Box.

Billy's room is near the far end of the hall. Just before knocking, Matthew can sense a presence. He turns to see Todd, also wearing a robe, standing behind him and smiling. "Hey Matt."

"Hey."

Todd is a year older than he and has just finished his freshman year at Harvard. When he started his initiation, Todd was chubby and awkward and reserved. But over the past few months he's trimmed down considerably and become popular with the other plebes. Matthew can see he's holding a DVD box. "I brought us some fun."

It's at this moment that Billy opens the door. "I thought I heard you guys out here." Billy is also in just a robe. He waves them inside. "Where's Baxter?"

Billy's room is very similar to Matthew's. There is heavy, old furniture and red velvet drapes gracing the windows. The only nod to modernity is the plasma screen and DVD player. But since Billy has been spending more time at the lodge, the space is taking on a few frat boy qualities. Dirty clothes are tossed casually on a chair. A mini refrigerator sits on the floor. A couple of sports posters are tacked to the walls.

"He can't make it; he's in trouble with his tutor."

"For what?"

"Damned is I know. He wouldn't tell me." Todd hands the DVD box to Matthew. "My brother loaned this to me for tonight. He says it's his favorite, a classic from the 70s." The cover features a sexy woman in her 20s with feathered blonde hair wearing a pink negligee. The porn's title is "Sex Games" and the tag line calls it "the ultimate computer fantasy."

"And this is a classic, too," Billy says holding up a bottle of rum. "From my dad's stock; He loves this shit mixed with Coke."

As Billy mixes the drinks, Todd takes the DVD from Matthew and inserts it into the player. "This should be good." Todd drops his robe to the floor. He still hasn't much muscle definition, but Matthew can see he's lost a lot of weight. Billy finishes the drinks and strips off his own robe. His body is well-defined, from abs to pecs to biceps. He grew up in a sports obsessed family and it shows. Billy hands each of them a glass and says to Matthew, "dude, relax." Matthew nods and slips off his own robe. The other boys chuckle at his briefs.

Todd holds up his glass in a toast. "To being life-long brothers." The other boys repeat the sentiment and drink. Matthew finds he likes the blend of sweet flavors.

Billy directs Matthew to the bed where he lies down in the middle, the other two boys on either side of him. The FBI warning fades from the screen and is replaced by fast clips of sex scenes and a toll-free number on the screen. "What the hell is that?" Billy asks.

"It's an ad," Todd grumbles. He tries pressing the menu button but a red dot flashes on the screen and the clips and the clips continue. One of them even has a midget fucking some blonde. "Now that's weird."

The commercial finally ends with the porn company's digital logo appearing on a field of stars. The actual movie begins with a shot of the credits being typed on an old, monochrome computer monitor. Billy takes another sip and asks, "dude, just how fucking old is this?"

"Late seventies."

On the screen, a sexy brunette with big, feathered hair is in her bathroom wearing nothing but a pink towel that she soon strips off. Todd gives a low whistle. "Look at those tits!" The woman is obviously getting ready for a night with her lover, putting on a red teddy and nylons.

Her lover is shown sitting in his robe in the living room. He is a lanky, handsome man with high cheekbones relaxing on a plaid sofa watching a porn tape. Everything about the room is very seventies, right down to the shag carpet. The woman appears and poses for him in her teddy before joining him on the sofa.

Matthew glances at the other boys and sees they are hard already. Todd is even lightly stroking himself. On the screen, the man makes his girlfriend squirm in delight as he eats her out through her red satin panties.

"You should be taking these off," Billy whispers as his hand slides under Matthew's waistband to touch his cock. "The fun is about to begin."

✶✶✶✶

Dinner at the mansion was a quiet affair. Only Patrick and Greg were there, eating in the casual family dining room off the kitchen. The nanny spent a little time with them, feeding baby Johnny from a bottle.

The only real conversation was about Richard Davis' arrest. "That girl," Greg grumbles, "seems to bring trouble to everyone she meets."

The meal is over and Patrick is upstairs in his room stretching out on his bed. He barely got any sleep last night and has been troubled all day about his discovery. He starts to doze off when his cell's ring pulls him back. It's Robert. *I should have expected this.* "Hey, Robert."

"I heard about your request. What's going on?"

Robert should no better. This is after all, a cell phone conversation. "It's something I have to explain in person."

"Does it have to do with Greg?"

"Yeah, sort of, but it affects a lot of other people. Why?"

"Because I got an email from him this morning; something big is going down, isn't it?"

Big doesn't begin to describe it. "Yeah, you could call it that."

"Then I'm flying in tomorrow."

EPISODE SEVEN

Greg Halloran is standing in the shower, arms folded, allowing the hot water to pummel his naked body.

His life seems to be stuck in neutral. Jack wants to have a future with him, especially as he deals with a grieving son. *But, do I really want that?* Julie will be back later today. He knows she'd like <u>them</u> to have a future, with <u>their</u> son, despite the deal they made months ago. He can easily see the three of them be a family again, here in the family homestead, and be happy. But he can see a similar fate with Jack and his boy. Little Jack might like having a baby brother, even if he's a stepbrother.

Turn left or turn right? This is the question that devils him. Whether Greg tries to concentrate on business or the Brothers legend or that bastard Mark Bradley, his mind keeps coming back to the same question: turn left or turn right. Even as he skin turns red and the bathroom fills with clouds of steam, he keeps asking himself *should I turn left or turn right?*

****

They have little to pack. Ann didn't expect to stay in Washington very long and Richard keeps enough clothes and items in the condo to not have to schlep much to Reagan National when travels between the capital and New Hampshire.

The packing is done in near total silence. They did not make love on their first night as a legally married couple. Richard called his daughter instead. Ann isn't sure what to say but knows that things won't be easy. Especially when she sees her husband pour himself an early morning scotch right before they leave. "Just one for the road," Richard explains.

****

Mrs. St. John left early this morning. Where she went or why, Denise hasn't a clue. She awoke alone and wandered through the penthouse until she came across a note written on ivory vellum in an elegant hand:

Denise

I must run some errands today. So much to do! Some men will
be coming by this morning to pack up everything for storage.
Be a dear and supervise. I'll be back sometime this afternoon.

Mrs. St. John

Only a few weeks ago, Denise was in awe of her sophisticated boss. But now she
shudders reading this note. Despite what Patrick Halloran says, she knows there
is more going on than just Julie's adoption. She simply needs to figure it out, and
do it in a way that doesn't cause Mrs. J to freak. Denise still cannot shake the
disturbing sight of that trashed living room.

A quick shower and a breakfast bar later, she starts to open drawers and cabinets.
Many of them are empty. Most of Mrs. St. John's wardrobe and jewelry are now
in Faraway Hill. The kitchen has dishes and cookware, of course, but there is
little food. Nor is anything odd or suspicious. She comes to the study. This
handsome, oak-paneled room is where Mr. St. John used to manage much of his
business affairs. These drawers are also empty, save for the occasional pen
or paperclip.

Denise wanders back to the living room, wondering where to look next. She spies
a little cabinet near the foyer. Opening it, she finds a year book from Faraway
Hill High School and photo album. She takes them with her to the sofa. Paging
through it she has a hard time finding anything of Mrs. J. But her photo is with
the rest of the graduating class:

Voted prettiest girl; voted most likely to succeed

The back pages are filled with the typical yearbook messages like "we'll miss
you" and "friends forever" and a particularly saucy "you are one hot babe!"
That's all, so Denise sets it aside and opens the photo album. It's all about Julie:
baby pictures, school pictures, letters to her favorite aunt --- a young woman's
life distilled in a collection of words and images.

As she flips through the pages, something falls to the floor. It's a snapshot of
four people taken in the garden behind the Halloran mansion. Denise studies
them for a moment and realizes that she knows three of them. These are Lewis
Halloran, Lorene Gale and Karen St. John back when they were young adults and
the future looked so bright. Lorene and Karen are in maids' uniforms and
everyone, smiling, looks like they've had a few too many. But the fourth man is a
mystery. Tall, athletic and handsome with a charming grin and bright eye that

sparkle for the camera. Turning it over, she sees written in Mrs. J's hand, "Lewis, Lorene and Alex with me" and a date.

About to go exploring again, Denise is stopped by the doorbell. The movers have arrived.

****

Turn left or turn right; that devilish question becomes more intimate and more powerful whenever Greg holds his son.

They are in the family dining room, he, Johnny, Patrick and the nanny. Breakfast is one of those few truly relaxed moments in a formal, historic home. Greg's omelet sits untouched on the plate as he cradles his boy, feeding him his morning bottle. Johnny looks up at his daddy with big brown, trusting eyes.

"He's doing quite well," the nanny says with her brogue as strong and charming as ever. "Why John seldom cries or give me a lick of trouble."

"No trouble, huh?" Patrick answers with a devilish grin. "That'll change; he's a Halloran, after all."

The nanny waves her hand as if to say "oh, you." Greg just smiles. It occurs to him that if he and Julie stay together they could give him a real brother. *Wouldn't that be cool?* That thought brings him back to a question he's wanted to ask his cousin. "Have you ever heard of the Brothers of Thebes?"

Patrick pauses, trying to look nonchalant. It's not working. "I don't think so, why?"

"Just some thing I found in dad's desk."

The young man nervously shrugs and takes a sip of his coffee, knowing full well that his cousin doesn't believe him.

****

The magnificent White Mountains slowly fade into the distance as the limo travels south back to Faraway Hill.

Unlike the lively trip to Bretton Woods, Julie and Agnes are quiet on the ride home. Julie isn't sure what the artist is thinking, but her mind keeps going back to her new brother, her two sets of parents and especially of her own son. It will be good to hold Johnny again.

"Penny for your thoughts," Agnes says watching Julie tap her fingers on the leather. "Although, with inflation and all, maybe I should say: a <u>quarter</u> for your thoughts."

Julie chuckles. "Oh, I've been going back and forth on everything."

"Everything is quite a lot."

"I have to make some decisions. Certain things have changed."

"Any idea what those decisions might be?"

"Well, I thought about something you said during the ride up."

"And what was that? I say so many, many wise things that I can't remember them all."

"About Greg, about how he may be a better friend to me than a husband."

"Oh, yes, I <u>was</u> being clever that day. What of it?"

"I think you're right, and I think I should stick to the plan I came up with months ago: to go forward with the divorce. Johnny and I will move into the building behind the mansion. This will allow us to be a family and still have our separate lives."

"That could mean Jack moving into the mansion."

"Yes, well, given a little time I think I can adjust to that. Besides, that's pretty simple compared to my other issues."

"Issues such as your mother and Karen."

"Yes; finding Eric changes things. I really can't wait much longer. But facing them will be one of the hardest things I've ever had to do."

****

There was a time when Ann avoided lunch at the Gale Farm. Munroe was usually morose, sometimes drunk and often stressed. During the lean years the mid-day meal would be nothing more than PB&Js. As she got older, Ann developed excuses so she could be somewhere else. But she has no excuse this time, and she is actually looking forward to being on the farm.

Her mother and Vivian have prepared a nice summer salad, with white meat chicken and loaded with fresh, tasty vegetables. Richard puts on the smooth charm that has made him such a success in politics. The women squeal with delight at being grandmothers with Richard explaining "that's what happened the other night, I was celebrating and got a little out of hand." Ann recognizes these words came directly from the press release. "My daughter, Rebecca is very happy for us." This lie is told well. In truth, Ann heard them argue on the phone last night.

Once lunch is over, Vivian offers to take Richard on a brief tour of the farm. He hasn't seen much of it in all the time they've been together. This leaves mother and daughter alone to clean-up. "Your father would have been thrilled," Lorene says as they fill the dishwasher. Ann knows she means Munroe.

"I guess."

"He was your father in every way that mattered."

"Mom, did you . . . did you ever regret marrying him?"

"No, not for a moment."

"Even when he was drunk?"

"He wasn't always drunk. And when he was sober, he was the sweetest man. Don't you remember that? Don't you remember any of the good times?" There were good times, more than she normally acknowledges. They include the trips to Rye and the little festivals across New Hampshire. Most of all, she remembers one when she was six. Suffering with flu on a cold winter's night, she couldn't sleep. Daddy stayed up with her, reading her stories and teaching her how to do a crossword until she fell asleep.

Ann kisses her mother on the cheek. "Yes, Mom, there were good times."

❊❊❊❊

Richard is trying to be gracious, but he's finding it exhausting. Vivian is walking him around the farm, showing him the improvements she and Lorene have been making. The barn has been expanded and painted; there are more cows now. But the humidity is getting to him and so is the growing urge for another scotch. "You both have done wonders" he says politely.

"Well, Lewis Halloran's bequest to Lorene paid for most of it. My late husband --- my second husband, that is, had a good life insurance policy. So we are doing quite well these days."

"I can see that."

"You don't seem to, though."

"What do you mean?"

"Here you are, newly married to a pretty and rich young girl with a baby on the way. You should be ecstatic."

"I am."

Vivian shakes her head. "No, you're not. I've been married twice; I know men. You are not happy, not really."

Richard didn't expect her to be so insightful, or is he too transparent? "It's just the surprise is all; I never expected to be a father again at my age."

"It's more than that. You have the face of a man with buyer's remorse."

I am too damned transparent.

"Look, Lorene and I know about Mark and his blackmail. I'm sure it's given you second thoughts about Annie. Don't let that young man ruin what could be a wonderful thing for you. This marriage and this baby are like a second life. I'm on my own second life right now, and trust me --- the second life is the best."

****

The crew is efficient. Denise needs to give them very little direction. Of the four men, three are the burly type in their 40s with beer bellies. But the fourth guy, whom Denise guesses is about 25, is pretty hot. He has a flat stomach, broad shoulders, tight ass and distinctive cheek bones. Best of all are his killer eyes, which sparkle whenever he smiles at her --- and he smiles at her a lot.

It's almost Noon and the men are preparing for their lunch break. With this efficiency, everything should be done by the end of the day. *Will we spend the night here,* she wonders, *or will Mrs. J book us a couple of hotel rooms?*

The kitchen is all packed up; boxes are sitting everywhere. But now that it's finished, it also gives her a private place to make the call she's wanted to make all morning. Denise pulls out her cell and presses a single button. Three rings and Jack answers: "hey, what's up?"

"We're packing."

"Come again?"

"Mrs. J says that we are relocating to Faraway Hill permanently."

"Shit."

"I think she's going to tell Julie the truth then all hell will break loose."

"When is this going down?"

"Right now; there is a crew here packing. Have you spoken to Patrick?"

"Not since getting his text, why?"

"Because there is more going on, I can feel it. And whatever it is, it's scary." She can hear Jack about to answer when a noise stops him. Denise can hear his son in the background, apparently waking from a nap.

"Sorry Dee, but we'll have to talk about this later."

Frustrated, she nearly throws her cell against the empty wall. "Is everything okay, ma'am?" She turns to see the hot mover, smiling and sparkling, as he stands at the kitchen's threshold. "Problems with the boyfriend?"

"I don't have a boyfriend. Where are the other guys?"

"Out having lunch."

"Aren't you hungry too?"

"Not for a cold turkey sandwich."

Denise smiles: this is a man who knows what he wants. She steps up to him and gives him a deep kiss. He wraps his arms around her to pull her tighter to him. A hand reaches down to caress her ass. Denise breaks their link long enough to ask "by the way, what's your name?"

"Brad."

"I'm Denise."

Brad reaches out for her but she steps back. With a sly grin, Denise slips her light summer dress to the floor, exposing her bare breasts and pink panties. Brad lets out a low whistle of appreciation. He quickly strips off his uniform, a standard brown shirt and pants. Denise marvels at his physique: not an ounce of fat, well-defined muscles and just a whiff of hair on his chest. She steps up intending to slide down his boxer briefs when Brad stops her. "Let me." He lifts Denise up with his powerful arms, gently sets her on the cold kitchen table and pulls off her pink panties. Then it happens: his tongue licks its way around the edge of Denise's pussy. She takes a deep breath when it reaches inside to seek out her labia. Brian plays with it the way a kitten would with a ball of string. Wave after wave of pleasure ripples through her body until finally she shakes from head to toe in orgasm.

Even before she can catch her breath, Denise can feel Brad's hard cock invade her. It feels bigger and thicker than she could have imagined. He is so turned on it only takes a few minutes until he cums, collapsing on top of her, panting.

"What great service your company provides," she says stroking Brad's damp hair. "I'll have to recommend you to all my friends."

****

There is little in the world less grand than lunch at a lawyer's office. But it's the most efficient place today, and Karen's daddy often praised efficiency as the most logical way to accomplish something.

So here she sits, in her attorney's office in the gleaming Time Warner Center, where they and her stepchildren review the complex documents over cold turkey sandwiches and bottled water. The overall deal is simple enough: Madeline and Jeffrey agree to purchase Karen's shares of the St. John Group at a premium once financing is in place. "According to my banker," Madeline explains, "we are only talking a few weeks; maybe sooner."

"I am so glad to hear that, dear." The three of them have never been this civil to each other. Even when Martin was alive, his children did little to hide their feelings about his wife.

Once everything is signed and initialed and notarized, Karen picks up her purse and waves them goodbye knowing that she'll never see the two of them again.

****

Meeting, meetings and more meetings: Patrick spends his day in one after the other. Greg is with him for most of them. They met with the director of the Faraway Hill mill about some equipment upgrades and the union contract negotiations coming up. A teleconference with the mill director in Georgia resolved small but frustrating issues. The sales staff needed to go over the materials for an upcoming trade show where buyers --- most of them fashion designers and retailers --- will be selecting cloth. The day will end with another teleconference, this time with the mill in Thailand.

This is what I went to college for? Patrick muses as he takes advantage of a slow moment to put his feet up on his desk and close his eyes. His thoughts begin to wander, and quickly they wander to Jessica, a hot little blonde he knew in artford. *Hmmm . . . I wonder if she'd come to Faraway Hill if I asked her.* These delicious memories of past hook-ups are interrupted by the phone. "Mr. Halloran," his secretary announces, "Robert Halloran is on Line 3." With a sigh, he picks up the receiver. "Hey, Robert."

"I've made the arrangements. Meet me at the Parker House tonight." *Fuck. He expects me to drive all the way to Boston.* "Why can't we meet in Manchester?"

"We need to be discrete. I think Greg is starting to get suspicious."

"He found some notes from Uncle Lewis about the Brothers. He's even asked me about them."

"Shit! Is that why you need to meet with the Elders?"

"No, what I have is way bigger --- way, way bigger."

****

Julie smiles at the limo pulls up under the portico. After more than a year of marriage, this big old house is finally starting to feel like home. Frederick is there to greet them with his gracious smile. "I trust you ladies had an enjoyable trip."

"We did; and how is Johnny?"

"He is doing quite well, Mrs. Halloran. The nanny is with him. I believe that it is nearly time for his afternoon nap." *Maybe I'll get a chance to hold him first.* Julie misses his big brown eyes looking up at her.

Now in her wheelchair and guided by a maid, Agnes follows her through the heavy doors and into the marble and gilt grand vestibule. Seeing it again makes Julie realizes that she is also starting to feel like the lady of the manor. Agnes notices this and winks at her.

****

"One must admire their efficiency," Karen exclaims upon her return. Nearly everything is packed up; so much so that she's decided to book them some rooms at the Plaza tonight. "That will make things much easier."

Denise smiles and follows her through the penthouse like an obedient puppy. Karen likes this; she likes being the focus. It should happen more often. "I have a delightful idea."

"What is that, Mrs. J?"

"For dinner, let's do take-out. It'll be fun, like an indoor picnic. The cable is still connected, isn't it?"

"Yes, ma'am."

"Chinese, let's do Chinese!" Karen gives her some cash and an order and shoos the girl out the door. Once Denise is gone, she takes a moment to reflect on the home she and Martin shared. That life is over. "Change is inevitable," her daddy used to say, "and logic says you should accept it, embrace it." Once back in Faraway Hill, Karen will start planning again. She needs to eliminate Greg Halloran. Some ideas are already simmering in the back of her mind. She simply needs to sit down and work out the details.

Karen's thoughts are interrupted by the chirp of her cell phone. *Such annoying things.* The screen indicates her sister is calling. *This should be fun.* "Hello, Eve, and how are you?"

"Fine."

"You must be feeling terribly lonely."

"There is a blurb on the Wall Street Journal's web site."

"Oh?"

"It says that there is a rumor going around about you selling Martin's company."

"My, the world is getting smaller."

"Then it's true."

"Yes, it is."

"Why would you do that?"

"Because I have decided to move back home permanently so that I can be with my daughter and my grandson."

"Damn it, Karen, this is just what I've warned you about."

"It's the right thing to do."

Eve says nothing. Karen can hear her sob through the phone. *Good; now you know how I felt when I gave up my little girl.* "You can't do this, it'll hurt her. It'll hurt me. Please Karen; I can't lose my daughter, too."

Karen is on the verge of laughing. Instead, she ends the call. *Soon, all will be as it should be.*

****

Turn left or turn right; the question has finally been answered. Shortly before dinner, Julie tells Greg about her trip to Bretton Woods and meeting her half-brother. "He's a nice young man; you'll like him." And that she will move forward with the divorce plan. "It's still the right thing for everyone."

He feels an odd mixture of guilt and relief. "I will always love you, Julie." She smiled and gave him a quick kiss. Then, still husband and wife, they walk down the mansion's Grand Staircase to the Blue Room where their guests are assembling for pre-dinner drinks. Agnes is here, with her daughter and grandson visiting. Bobby has really grown since the last time Greg saw him. *He's going to break a few hearts.* Eve is here, too, to welcome her daughter home and to spend a little time later with Johnny. Greg notices how stressed she looks. *Losing Ben must be so hard for her.* The fact that he, too, could have died in the same fire has him realizing that Julie is right: they need to live their lives.

Patrick is in Boston, meeting with friends.

Only two people are missing and Greg doesn't mind their absence. The moment of peace is short lived as Frederick announces "Senator and Mrs. Davis" before ushering in Ann and her husband. She is all smiles but he is more subdued. Greg suspects Richard has been having his own cocktail hour.

"I have some exciting news," she announces with no small amount of pride. "Richard and I are having a baby."

****

Patrick looks out the window where he can see people gather in Boston Common for a free nighttime concert in the park.

"I had to take that call," Robert tells him without an apology as he sets his cell on the handsome cherry wood table next to the file box. They on the fourteenth floor of the historic Parker House, in the suite named for the legendary hotel's original owner. "Now what's in the box that's so damned important?"

Patrick steps over to the table and lifts the lid. "These are Karen St. John's project plans."

"Project plans?"

He hands Robert one of the folders. "These are copies. I found the originals in her house."

Looking skeptical, Robert skims the carefully typed papers, some with handwritten comments in an elegant scrawl. "Holy shit, is this for real?"

Patrick nods and sighs, "She poisoned Uncle Lewis and Aunt Lilly."

"She's so damned methodical. Even how she seduced that boy cop in Faraway Hill; step by step."

"There is a lot more in there, about how she killed her husband and tried to kill Greg. Speaking of which, I just found out something about Julie."

"I can guess," Robert frowns has he reaches for another folder. "Karen Scott is Julie's biological mother."

"You knew?"

"Kid, I was around when the shit happened. Julie's real dad is a close friend of Lewis'."

"He's still alive?"

"Damned right he's still alive --- and I know just where to find Alexander Mundy."

EPISODE EIGHT

Denise wants to close her eyes and drift into a welcoming slumber. Normally it should be easy to fall asleep in a big comfy First Class seat. The rumble of the jet's engines often helps. But this morning is different. Despite a long, exhausting night, anxiety keeps Denise from nodding off. She's starting to feel like the victim of a kidnapper or a cult leader, blindly following a dangerous woman wherever she wants to go.

Mrs. J kept her awake until the wee hours making Denise watch old movies on cable before jumping into a cab for the Plaza. She hasn't stayed up that late in more than a year, when she and some friends went clubbing through Manhattan. That night she hooked up with a hot bartender named Jeff Something. The tedium of Mrs. J raving about ancient glamour girls like Lana Turner and Rosalind Russell were more exhausting than any college party.

"Stewardess," Mrs. J says, taking the seat next to her. "Be sure to bring me a mimosa once we're in the air. Would you like one, too, dear?"

Denise shakes her head. "No, thanks." Closing her eyes, she tries to think about yesterday afternoon and Brad. Fucking him was the best part of her entire trip. But the reality of her situation can't be ignored.

"Oh, Denise, I am so looking forward to being in Faraway Hill."

The plane takes off, pushing the passengers back in their seats. The belt holding Denise may as well be ropes that have strapped her to a chair. This kidnapping may be luxurious, but it's still a kidnapping of sorts.

How the fuck can I get away from this crazy lady?

****

Little Jack sits at the table, swirling his Cocoa Puffs with a spoon, creating a chocolate soup. He is not smiling. His eyes are not sparkling. He just sits there, staring at the bowl and the things his spoon is doing to it.

"Come on, buddy, it's your favorite." No response. Jack is worried about him. Last night his son woke up screaming for his papa. He held the boy in his arms until he cried himself back to sleep.

Jack's cell rings. It's Greg calling. "Hey Jack, how's it going?" *He sounds happy. I wonder why.* He glances at his morose little boy and answers cautiously, "as well as things can be, I suppose."

"Well, I have some news." Jack's heart sinks with dread: *he's going back to his wife. I guess that I can't blame him.* "Julie and I talked things over before dinner last night. We've agreed to go ahead with the divorce plans." *Fuck, yeah!*

"That is so cool, dude. When can we get together?"

"Hopefully tonight. I'll text you later today."

****

The fresh plaster; the new windows; the original hardwood floors and the sturdy redbrick: everything about the old servants' building symbolizes what Julie Halloran is doing with her life. For the first time in months, she feels as if her world is starting to stabilize again.

"Mrs. H., I can do wonders with this place!" Eduardo enthuses as he roams excitedly from room to room, upstairs and down. Eduardo was recommended by Karen, who found him serving big name clients in Boston. He is a short, fey little man who was actually born in South Boston with the less interesting name Bernard Brannon.

"Good, because I want my guests to feel comfortable and my aunt speaks well of you." Julie isn't telling anyone just yet about her real plans for the house. She needs to sit down with her mother first, and people in small towns like Faraway Hill gossip way too much.

"Oh, I just love Mrs. St. John. She's very classy, very stylish. I'm looking forward to redoing her living room."

"I don't understand, didn't you just redo the entire house?"

"Yes, several months ago. *Boston Magazine* did a really nice write-up. But then I get this call a few days ago from her assistant. When I visited the entire room had been emptied. It was very strange, but then, truly creative people can be very eccentric. I guess she just wanted a change."

****

Talk about the idle rich: Ann spends her morning trying to fill not hours but minutes. She wanders from room to room but there is nothing to do in any of them. Back at the farm she could lose herself in housework. But the housekeeper handles all of that at Four Corners. She tried reading, but none of the esoteric books in Richard's library interest her. And, of course, she has no real friends to call.

Most bothersome of all is Richard. He skipped breakfast and is sitting on the back porch, staring at the trees, sipping one drink after another. Ann is starting to wonder if she's made the same mistake her mother made in marrying Monroe.

Finally, she plops onto the sofa and turns on the TV. She flips through the channels. There is nothing much to watch. She stops at MSNBC to watch Andrea Mitchell announce that "New Hampshire Senator Richard King and his new, and very young wife, are expecting their first child."

Ann glances at the phone. When news gets out about a pregnancy, most women can expect calls from friends and acquaintances. But the landline and her cell remain silent.

They remain silent all day.

****

Greg is starting to feel good about his life. Ann is out of the mansion permanently. He and Julie have become friends; they and their son can remain a family even while living apart. Soon he'll have Jack back. Things are coming together.

There is only one thing that continues to gnaw at Greg, and he isn't sure why. He again puts in a late morning call to California --- which is three hours behind him --- and again Robert's assistant gives Greg the usual runaround. Robert's silence and Patrick's evasions have convinced him that there may be something to the Brothers legend.

If only he can find out.

****

The café is just off Elm Street, not far from the charred remains of King's Korner. Jack and his son stroll down the sidewalk. Little Jack struggles to carry his overnight bag, bulging with clothes, books and a few toys. More than once Jack has offered to carry it for him, but his son emphatically insists that "I can do it!"

At least he's talking, Jack consoles himself. The boy's continued reticence worries him. Fortunately, the news that he gets to spend a couple of nights with Chloe has cheered him a little. It makes Jack feel better too; he can take a break from the trauma of Joe's death while, hopefully, reconnecting with Greg the way they have in the past.

The café is a little place below street level, accessed by some old stone steps. Inside is a cozy room crowded with chairs and tables. People are sitting and chatting or surfing the wifi or munching on some sweet treat. A brick wall dominates one side and a simple, white wall the other. It is here they find Chloe, standing on a stool, adjusting a painting. The café has agreed to display some of her works in exchange for a commission on any sale. "Hey guys!"

A rare smile brightens Little Jack's face. "I know that Jack's been looking forward to this," his father says.

"Me, too; Aaron is putting in some extra hours and I hate to be alone. Say, dude, you like chocolate chip cookies? They have the best here and I get a discount. Go ask for one at the counter." The boy looks up to Jack for permission, which is provided with a nod and a smile. "You know," he whispers to Chloe, "I really appreciate your doing this."

"Hey, I like the kid --- and you, too. How are things going?"

"Last night was tough. He woke up crying for his papa. It worries me."

"I know it's not my place to say, but maybe you should consider some therapy."

The thought has crossed Jack's mind. "Maybe, but how do you explain our weird situation to a therapist?"

"Beats me; but I don't think you have any other choice."

****

"Oh, how good it is to be home."

The simple flight to Manchester turned into a complex and frustrating series of mishaps. First, the plan exhibited engine trouble forcing them to return to New York. After more than an hour waiting in the cabin, the passengers were finally allowed to disembark. Another three hours were spent at the airport, eating lunch and waiting for a new flight. Things seem to finally go well; that plane took off on time without any problems. Then a bomb scare (it turned out to be a hoax) in Boston forced the plane to circle for another two hours. At last they were able to land at Manchester International.

It's getting a bit much for Denise.

"Oh my," Mrs. J says looking around her empty living room. "It seems Eduardo hasn't even started yet." Denise wonders how the lady can compartmentalize her strange actions. "Well, be sure to call him in the morning, dear."

"Yes, ma'am," this gives Denise the opportunity to excuse herself and walk back to her little apartment. At first, Faraway Hill seemed to Denise like a hick town,

then a charming little village and now a frightening place that only someone like
Rod Serling could have dreamed up. Coming up to the town square, she gazes at
the statute of John Halloran. It always impresses her how much Greg looks
like him.

And it makes her wonder what strange thing will happen next to them all.

****

Gravel crunches beneath the tires as Julie guides her Lexus up the driveway. She
comes to a stop, turns off the engine and a takes a moment to peer through the
windshield. Before her is her childhood home. Julie remembers being a little girl,
maneuvering around workmen and piles of lumber while the place was
renovated. She remembers the late night talks with her mother and being picked
up for the prom by Dennis Grant in his ill fitting rented tux. These memories
make Julie feel good about herself and her life.

Her mother greets her at the door with a smile. "I'm glad you came by." Julie can
tell that she's been crying. Her eyes are a little puffy and her cheeks red.

"Mom, if you're having a tough time, you're always welcome at our place."

"I know, but I'm fine."

Julie follows her into the living room and sees an old, opened file box with books
and papers scattered across the coffee table. "What's all this?"

"It was your father's; well, actually, it belonged to his family. I never really
looked at them before." The two sit together on the sofa. A moldy scent gently
floats from the box. "Did you know," she says handing Julie a document, "that
the family's original name was Kingsmythe?"

She looks at the birth certificate. It's from England and dated July 12, 1901 for a
baby named Arthur Kingsmyth. "I never knew that."

"From what I can see, at some point the Kings worked as blacksmiths for the
royal court. I guess when they emigrated they just shortened the name."

Julie's studies the papers. Her father seldom spoke about his ancestors, or even
his own parents. "Mom, we need to talk."

"Sure; what about?"

Julie knows that she needs to be delicate, diplomatic. "I had the best childhood,"
she prefaces with a soft smile. "And I had the best parents. All of my friends told
me so."

Eve reaches over and squeezes her daughter's hand. "You made it pretty easy."

"Oh, I doubt that," Julie laughs.

"Well, maybe 'easy' is the wrong word; but you were worth it. Why bring this up now?"

"Because," Julie answers slowly and carefully, "when Greg and I came over to get the insurance documents we . . . We found my birth certificate and adoption papers."

Eve freezes, her face locked in stunned, fearful silence. Julie can even feel the grip of her hand tightening. "As far as I'm concerned, <u>you</u> are my mother not Karen."

"Oh, thank God," Eve answered, smiling and relieved. "You mean that, don't you?"

"Of course I do. Don't get me wrong, I love Aunt Karen and I'd like to know more about the man who --- well, the point is that being a mother myself I understand that there is more to it than just giving birth."

"I wish your father was here. He would love to hear that."

"Me, too; but, Mom, there is more. Much more."

"Has Karen spoken to you?"

"No, why?"

"She sold Martin's company and told me on the phone yesterday that she's going to tell you who your mother really is."

"<u>You</u> are my real mother. Nothing she says can change that."

"Then what else is there?"

"Up in Bretton Woods, while there with Agnes, I met a nice young man. His name is Eric . . . Eric Mundy."

"You mean ---"

Julie nods. "He's my kid brother."

"What a strange coincidence. Does he know about you?"

"Yes, and we are going to try to have a friend ship."

"Does he know what happened to Alex?"

"No one seems to; I'm beginning to think he may be dead."

There is one more thing she must tell her. In the same careful, diplomatic fashion, she explains the situation with Greg. This is something Julie has spent some time rehearsing. She lays out the timetable: the issue of Ann, the strain it put on their marriage, Greg reconnecting with Jack. She even tells her about Jack and his son.

"This is unbelievable! I can't believe Greg is gay. There were stories about all those girls ---"

"Most of those stories are true, but there were a few guys in the mix."

"You must be devastated."

"I was, at first; but so much has happened in the past year. Do you know, despite everything, how he has stuck with me through each crisis?"

Eve nods. "I remember how he acted at your accident and Johnny's birth. He was so supportive when your father died. That's why I can't believe he doesn't love you."

"He does, but he loves Jack, too. It was Agnes said something to me that makes a lot of sense."

"What is that?"

"Greg makes a better friend for me than a husband."

****

The darkest, most painful moments of Ann's childhood all involve Munroe. Every time something went wrong, or didn't work out as he wanted, the man she called Dad for over twenty years dealt with them the same way. He'd walk down to Murphy's General Store in Faraway Hill's main square and purchase some bourbon or some beer (whichever he could afford). Munroe would then find some secluded place on the farm and drown himself.

He ruined birthdays and graduations and so many other important moments in Ann's life. She couldn't bring friends (what few she had) or boyfriends to the house. She endured endless gossip about the Gales with people all over town whispering about Munroe's drinking or Lorene's weight gain or the farm's mortgage or Ann's latest embarrassment.

Ann had convinced herself that those days ended when her father swallowed a bottle of poison. But now she finds herself living through it again. Only this time, she's not the daughter; she's the wife.

Richard didn't bother to come to dinner. He stayed in his study. The housekeeper was given the day off, so Ann ordered some Italian delivered to the house. Ann ate quietly, in front of the TV, watching some old movie. She fell asleep, waking up a few hours later. Richard was still in his study. Ann opened the door a crack. He was passed out on the leather sofa, a half empty bottle of scotch on the table.

This is when she makes her decision.

With tears streaming down her cheeks, Ann climbed the stairs to the master bedroom. She packs up her clothes and carries the luggage back down to the living room. She writes the following note:

Dear Richard

I love you more than you can know. But I realize that my past mistakes have hurt you. They've hurt me, too. I didn't plan on Mark coming back or even do what he did. But it happened and I'm sorry.

I also think my pregnancy has you feeling trapped. I'm sorry about that, too. But I love this baby as much as I love you. I want both of you.

But I grew up with a father who drowned his problems. I won't have a husband who does the same thing. I saw up close how Munroe hurt my mother. I can't be like her and I can't have our child grow up that way.

I once told you that I'm New Hampshire's most scandalous woman. I suppose leaving you this way and at this time means another scandal. Maybe I should get used to the scandals. But I don't see any other option.

Should you decide to make a change and stop drinking and
try to make our little family work, then call my cell.
Otherwise I can't deal with this pain anymore.

Love from your wife,
Ann

She leaves the note where Richard is sure to find it --- on the bar --- picks up her
luggage and leaves Four Corners, hoping and praying that there is still one man
she can count on.

****

There is one man he can count on. It hasn't always been this way, but Greg
knows that things have changed. Both he and Jack have grown enough and
matured enough. They are no longer college kids goofing off after class or
chasing tail over the weekend. Today they are grown men and fathers.

There is only one woman he can truly count on. Greg realizes that, too, after all
he and Julie have been through. She is the best friend he's ever had.

When he meets Jack for dinner, it's relaxed and fun. The men choose Maxwell's,
the same restaurant Greg took him to on Jack's first visit. They swap tales of
college and old times and both of them flirt with Debbie. A private little joke
begins between them and continues through the meal about ways of tempting the
sexy waitress into a threesome.

After dinner, the two men stroll together through the warm evening. Manchester
seems so calm in the still air. There are other people out for the evening. Not
many, but a few.

They enter Jack's old apartment. Neither of them wants to make love in Joe's
bed. Doing so seems wrong. They haven't been here together since watching
Mark Bradley's blackmail video. The place looks even less lived-in than before,
with more furniture and photos moved to the other apartment. Greg wonders
when Jack will give up renting two homes.

There is no discussion, no preliminaries. The two men walk directly into the
bedroom. Clothes are tossed to the floor and Greg marvel's at his lover's incredible body. Despite the tumult in recent weeks, Jack has somehow maintained the
same physique first mapped out in college.

They make out for the longest time, caressing each other's chest and stroking
each other's cock. Eventually, Jack whispers "I want you inside me."

A little bit of lube and Greg enters him, with Jack's legs hooked over Greg's shoulders. He stops for a moment, relishing the warmth and tightness. He looks at Jack's face and sees a blissful smile. Greg begins the piston motion, in and out, in and out, while his lover rolls his head left and right. He wants to make this moment last, but passion overtakes him and Greg picks up the pace until, finally, he cums inside Jack.

Panting and sweating, Greg starts to pull out when Jack stops. "Wait; stay like that." With Greg's cock still inside him, he jerks himself off until his stomach and chest are sprayed with cum. Greg wipes up some of it with his finger, tastes it with a smile, then leans in --- cock still in ass --- leans over and kisses him.

****

There is something quaint about sitting on the front porch. Karen has never really appreciated it until tonight. She is sitting on an expensive rocker, a notepad on her lap and a glass of wine at her side. Every so often people stroll by. They smile and they wave. Karen can recognize most of them. They were people she knew as a girl, growing up in Faraway Hill with a widowed mother and an older sister. Back then she dreamed of leaving, of getting out and seeing the world. Karen has seen the world. And now she's home again.

Taking another sip of the merlot, she returns her attention to the notepad. She is trying to come up with an idea that will finally make things right. Ben is dead, Mark is gone and Eve cannot stop her. All that remains is coming up with a logical plan to kill Greg Halloran. But after two frustratingly failed attempts, Karen has run into a brick wall.

And then an idea: *why not keep it simple?* Her associate in Boston can make it happen. She starts drafting her project plan. First, the goal, then each step one after the other. It will look like a common, every day car accident. Karen smiles satisfied that this will work. In the morning, she will formally type the project plan on her laptop and place it in her special file box.

****

"The trip to Claremont really wore him out," Peter's mother whispers. They are standing just outside in the master bedroom, watching his father snore. He remembers the man being so strong, so energetic. He'd spend a long day at the Halloran mill creating fabric to be used in clothes across the country. Yet, no matter how tired, he also came home with a smile or a joke or even a little song. Sometimes he'd stop by Hugh's Bar but only for a brief drink with his buddies. Family mean too much to him.

"I though you both enjoyed it."

"Oh, we did. And he was in such good spirits the whole time. But I guess it was too much for him." Peter can see his mother is tired, too. He can also see how much his parents have aged. They had him late, after nearly 20 years of marriage, a surprise and welcome pregnancy. His birth was a moment of joy.

They can hear a slight knock coming from the foyer. Peter suspects who their late visitor is and kisses his mother goodnight and leaves her to prepare for bed. Strolling down the hall he becomes more and more convinced who is there. And he's right: there she stands, on the outside of the locked screen door, a sad look on her face and an overnight bag sitting on the porch. "Hello, Mrs. Davis."

"Peter, please, I need you."

"Sorry, I don't offer that kind of service. Try your ex-husband. Maybe he'll give you a discount."

"Damn it," tears start rolling down her cheeks. "I've left Richard. He's home, in that big fucking house, passed out drunk in the living room."

Peter can see the pain in her eyes. It's almost as searing as the pain in his heart. "You can't come in. My parents are home."

"Where am I supposed to go?"

"Go to your mother's place."

"I can't; she and Vivian have gone to bed by now."

"Then go back to your fancy suite in the big house."

"I can't deal with the Hallorans, not like this; I can't handle that humiliation."

"Then, go to a hotel or a B&B here in town or even Manchester."

"You know that's not an option. The moment I check into some place rumors will start spreading all over the state."

"Why are you bitching? Growing up, this is the life you always wanted: to be rich and famous. You got your wish Mrs. Davis. Congratulations: you're now so rich and famous you've got nowhere to go."

✼✼✼✼

The black car with tinted windows travels down one winding road after another. Patrick, in the back seat, is nervous. He's doing something tonight he never expected to do.

Robert grumbles. He is sitting next to Patrick, focused on his iPad. Something makes him unhappy, probably a business deal gone wrong. Robert seems to live for business; Patrick has never known him to date or do anything purely social. He turns back to the window, but still can't see anything. The tinted windows are almost solid black at night. It doesn't matter, though, as the Brothers' lodge is well hidden. Located out in the Massachusetts hinterland, it cannot be found on any map. It has no address, no markings. A car's onboard computer won't know anything about it. Nothing appears on Mapquest. All that Google Earth will display are the tops of trees. The lodge officially does not exist.

The quiet, two-hour trip ends with the car pulling up to the gate, being buzzed in, and stopping before the huge, gothic stone building. Patrick and Robert emerge from the car without saying a word. They both know why they are here. What they don't know, at least not for sure, is what will happen.

Carved above the big oak doors is the official name: *Sanctus Frater of Thebes.* Surprisingly, the men are greeted by their cousin, Matthew, who is on door duty tonight. The young man looks sharp in the standard plebe attire of simple black pants and white oxford shirt.

"Es vos meus frater?" Matthew asks the required formal question, forgetting that it should be plural. Patrick and Robert give the correct response, causing the recent prep school graduate to blush at his realization.

Matthew ushers them into a privileged and exclusive world. Women are only allowed rarely and for limited, specific reasons. This is a masculine domain, one of carved wood paneling, rare artwork, secrets and ceremonies that are strictly male.

"How are things?" Patrick whispers to him.

"Okay, what's up? Matthew whispers back.

Robert loudly clears his throat, signaling that the conversation needs to end.

The major domo emerges from his office. He is a stout man, balding, and yet has an air of natural and confident dignity. They exchange formal greetings in Latin. "The Elders have been briefed. Please, brothers, follow me." An elevator takes them down into the lodge's most secure floor, an inner sanctum that Patrick has never seen. The doors slide open to reveal a space so different, it could be another building. Gone are the heavy oak furniture, paneled walls and plush, Oriental rugs. They are now in a land of marble: the walls, floors and even the ceiling of this antechamber glisten with light from brass chandeliers and sconces.

The major domo leads them to a pair of huge, ornate brass doors. He knocks. A voice from inside asks a question in Latin and the stout man responds appropriately. He then opens the door to escort the Hallorans inside where Patrick sees yet another magnificent marble room, this one complete with impressive columns. The ambience has a distinct Greco-Roman feel; Patrick half expects to see pretty young slaves in scanty togas bringing libations for the master's guests.

Instead what dominates the room is a large table, also carved in marble. Seven men are seated here, three on each side and one at the head. Robert is about to present the required Latin greeting when the man at the head waves him aside. "We can dispense with the formalities." He points to the two empty chairs at the other end of the table. "Please, sit down, brothers."

Each footfall echoes through the chamber as the cousins walk up to the table and take their seats. The chairs are hard with no cushions; the back ram-rod straight. It makes Patrick feel a little like he's been called to the headmaster's office after being caught in some prank.

"Brother Robert already knows who we are," explains the man. "But allow me to introduce everyone to you, young man." Patrick can now get a good look at him and the others. He must be about 80, lean and wrinkled yet he wears his dignity as comfortably as a well-tailored suit. "I am Senior Elder George Adams."

"Hello, sir."

"To my right is Elder Andrew Hamilton," another old man with natural grace. "Next to him is Elder James Jefferson," Patrick has heard of him. He is one of the few African-Americans to become brothers and the first to become an Elder. "And that gentleman is Elder Delmar Jackson," a bit younger than the other two, Elder Jackson looks to be in his sixties. Elder Adams introduces the three other men, all white and advanced in years: Elder John Washington, Elder George Hancock and Elder Thomas Revere.

Having finished the introductions, Elder Adams returns his gaze to the Halloran cousins. "We have all been briefed on the situation involving the St. John woman and her crimes against the Brothers. However, we have a . . . an unusual problem with delivering the necessary justice."

Patrick looks at Robert, who doesn't seem surprised. *Why can't they just dispatch an Enforcer? That's how they got rid of Mel Waite.*

Elder Adams sees the confusion in his face. "You see, young man, our best Enforcer has a tie with the woman in question. He has declined to deliver justice in the usual manner." *Declined? Since when can an Enforcer refuse an order? And why not just have another one do it?*

"By the very nature of their position," explains Elder Jefferson, "the Enforcers have developed their own brotherhood within the Brothers."

Robert remains silent; the Quiet Halloran lives up to his reputation. So it's Patrick who asks, "I don't understand. What can we do?"

"Perhaps this will help," Elder Adams motions to the major domo, who steps out. "Normally we would send an Enforcer to remove her, as we have others who have harmed Brothers. But as I explained, this situation is quite different."

The major domo returns. Joining him is a handsome man in his late 40s or early 50s, with the lithe frame of an athlete, the confident walk of a man who knows his place in the world, and streaks of grey adding a rich dimension to his hair.

"Brother Patrick Halloran, meet Brother Alexander Mundy."

EPISODE NINE

Patrick is surprised by the time. He's normally an early riser but he had nodded off the moment his head hit the pillow and woke much later than usual. It was a deep, dreamless sleep as if his brain was recovering from what is surely the weirdest moment of Patrick's young life.

Last night, Alexander Mundy made his proposal to the Elders. The plan will punish and neutralize Karen St. John without killing her. The Elders' approved unanimously. Patrick voiced his reluctant support. Robert merely nodded. It was interesting how quiet the Quiet Halloran became after Mundy appeared.

Since it was so late, the Halloran cousins slept at the lodge.

After a quick shower, Patrick heads down to the dining room. Robert is sitting at the table, an empty plate before him, sipping his coffee and reading today's *New York Times.* This is the hardcopy paper, not the iPad. All such devices must be kept with the major domo until the brother departs.

"Good morning."

Robert grunts his response. The plebes on breakfast duty are busy clearing the table, but one manages to bring Patrick a plate of scrambled eggs and toast along with some orange juice. He takes his first bites when someone else enters the room.

"Good morning Bob."

Patrick and Robert turn to see Alex Mundy standing near them, a friendly smile on his face. He has never heard anyone call Robert anything other than Robert. The man's discomfort is so obvious it's almost comical. Patrick stifles a chuckle; it's good to see his often arrogant cousin humbled a little.

"Hello, Alex," Robert responds briskly. He folds up his paper, stands and informs Patrick that they will be leaving soon.

"That's a shame, Bob; I was hoping we could catch up on old times."

Saying nothing and looking embarrassed, Robert leaves the room. Alex takes his recently vacant seat and explains "Bob and I were plebes together. We went through the orientations and initiations."

"I didn't know."

"He took things too seriously. I saw us as brothers and fuck buddies. He . . . well, he saw us as something more." *So Robert fell in love and had his heart broken*. Patrick almost feels sorry for him.

"I noticed last night," Alex asks him, "that you weren't all that thrilled with the plan I came up with."

"It's alright --- but way better than what she deserves."

"Maybe, but I can't do that to my daughter. Julie has lost too much as it is."

"So you keep on eye on her."

"I check in from time to time and see how my kids are doing."

"Kids?"

"I also have a son. By a lucky coincidence they met recently. I'm glad too; Eric hasn't had much family since his mother died."

Alex is a surprise. Patrick always assumed that Enforcers are cold, efficient tools doing whatever the Elders assign them. But here is a man who is thoughtful, even gentle. There is nothing weak about him. Not in his build or his gait. But the lines of his face reveal a man who has experienced a lifetime of loss and grief, a man who has gained a sort of wisdom.

"So, Brother Patrick, how does it feel to no longer be a plebe?"

"A relief; the classes were bad enough, but initiations got . . . weird."

"Like the final one?" he asks with a knowing smirk.

"<u>Especially</u> the final one."

Alex glances about them and then leans in to whisper, "I shouldn't tell you this, but I was part of your final initiation."

"You were?"

"It was hot, it always is."

Patrick says nothing; part of him still feels humiliated by the experience. Alex notices this and points out that "every man in that room --- including me --- went through the same thing."

"I know."

"Trust me, being a Brother is worth it. A lot of doors are opening for you."

"Well, I'm a Halloran. I didn't have much choice."

"Your cousin Greg is a Halloran and his mother kept him from joining."

"True."

"Do you think he was cheated?"

Patrick has been asking himself the same question. "Yes, in a way, I do."

"Then maybe I can help correct that."

****

The high pitch sound jolts Jack awake. He tries to ignore it, but it happens again. He left the cell on in case Chloe needs to contact him. Now he's starting to regret that.

Greg, lying next to him, begins to stir. Jack has to reach over his naked lover to pick up the phone. But the name on the screen isn't Chloe. Its Jack's little brother. "Hey, Nick, what's up? Why the fuck are you calling so damned early?"

"Sorry dude, but I had no choice. I've got some big news for you."

****

Ann slowly opens her eyes to see Brad Pitt staring back at her.

It takes Ann a moment to get her bearings. Brad is actually a poster, one of many, covering the rose wallpaper in Julie's childhood bedroom. She also sees a menagerie of stuffed animals from giraffes to monkeys. These charming creatures with their charming smiles are propped on the mock Queen Anne dresser and the mock Queen Anne desk. This is a girl's room with all the fun things girls collect. Growing up, Ann wanted her room to be more like Julie's, but Munroe couldn't afford it. It was one of the reasons she always enjoyed sleepovers at the Kings'. The other, of course, was that they always seemed like such a happy and loving family. Alcohol and poverty and buried issues didn't hover over them as they did the Gales.

After a quick trip to the bathroom, Ann slips into her robe and goes downstairs. The pleasant aroma of recently brewed coffee greets her just before entering the kitchen. Mrs. King, dressed for the office, smiles warmly. "Good morning."

"Good morning." She's grateful for Julie's mother. Ann ran out of options last night. Driving past the King home, she saw the lights still on. Mrs. King welcomed her without hesitation and without questions. "I really appreciate your letting me stay here, Mrs. King."

Mrs. King hands her a warm mug filled with fresh brew. "You are welcome; and I think your old enough now to call me Eve."

"Thanks, Eve." Ann takes a sip and realizes that this is the same blend Eve and Julie used to serve in their little shop.

"Actually, I probably should be thanking you. This big house feels a lot bigger these days. Are you ready to talk about what happened?"

Ann considers the offer for a moment and realizes that she needs to confide in someone. Normally that would be Julie, but Julie isn't here. "My marriage is in trouble, big trouble."

"How can that be? Your still newlyweds and you've got a baby on the way."

"I also had an unwelcome guest at my wedding."

"Who?"

"Mark."

Eve stiffens at the sound of his name. *Why would she do that? What is Mark to her?* "I can't believe that bastard just showed up at your wedding."

"Well, he did and he had news: we weren't really divorced. He blackmailed my attorney into giving me fake papers. While on our honeymoon Richard's lawyer confirmed everything."

"I can't believe that Richard Davis, of all people, would hold that against you."

"Not at first. In the beginning he was so amazing. Richard was my hero. He made all the arrangements to get the divorce and get rid of Mark."

"Then, I don't understand."

"Everything changed the day Richard met Mark to pay him off. I don't know what was said or what happened, but ever since I can sense Richard regrets ever marrying me. Now, with the pregnancy, he feels trapped. So trapped, he's starting to drink. He reminds me so much of Munroe."

A tear crawling down her cheek, a sympathetic Eve sets down her mug to wrap her comforting arms around her. "That boy has hurt so many people."

****

It isn't even Noon yet and already Julie can sense that it's going to be a scorcher. Dressed in shorts and a tank top, she braves the climbing temperature walking from the Halloran mansion into Faraway Hill proper.

People she's known all her life wave at her, or stop to briefly chat. Even the tourists are friendly. Julie's grateful not only for their kindness, but for the delays these pleasant exchanges provide. The weather may be sizzling, but it doesn't compare to the heat she's about to endure.

Stepping two blocks from the main square she stops outside a beautiful old house, a former bed & breakfast that Karen St. John has turned into her home. The wrap-around porch is especially nice. It looks like the kind of ideal home found in a classic novel or movie. Even the rose bushes look Hollywood perfect.

Julie takes a deep breath, screws up her courage and walks up to the door. Karen opens the door only seconds after hearing the bell. "Hello, dear," she greets her with a lovely smile. "Please come in."

Karen escorts her into the living room which, much to Julie's surprise, has nothing but a pair of folding chairs and a card table. "I'm replacing the furniture," her aunt explains.

"That's what Eduardo told me. But I thought you liked the furniture. You even had the room photographed."

"I just felt like a change. Would you like some lemonade? You look parched." Julie could use something to drink, although the air conditioning by itself is a welcome relief. "I'll have to get it myself. Denise is running errands for me in Manchester."

While Karen is in the kitchen, Julie scans the living room. She misses the big painting of Lake Winnipesauke that hung over the mantle. *Why would she get rid of that?* Looking around, Julie is starting to notice a few other oddities. Little pieces of fabric, forgotten by a hasty vacuum, lie next to the fireplace. As she steps over to take a closer look, a tiny piece of glass snaps beneath her feet. *This is really strange. That fabric looks like it came from her sofa.*

"I hope that you like it," Karen says, returning to the living room with a tray in her hands. "It's sugar free; we need to watch our waists, after all. Is something wrong?"

Julie shakes her head. "Everything is fine." The two women sit in the folding chairs. Karen pours them each a glass. The cold, refreshing liquid rejuvenates Julie. "Aunt Karen, you are my favorite person."

Karen smiles a smile that, to Julie, looks like the kind of practiced smile winners wear when receiving an Academy Award.

"You've brought so much to my life, stories of New York, help with fashion and boys. You have been the greatest aunt any girl could want."

"Thank you, Julie. But what's this all about?"

Julie takes another long drink. "A few weeks ago . . . I found my birth certificate."

Karen's face brightens with the joy of a woman whose greatest dreams have suddenly come true. "I am so very happy! We can now be a real family, you, me and Johnny."

"Pardon?"

"You both can move in here, I have plenty of room."

Oh my God, what is she talking about? "Aunt Karen, I love you very much. And even though you gave birth to me, I already have a mother."

The joy is gone. Karen's face hardens. She stares at Julie with a pair of cold eyes. "I don't understand."

"I love you," Julie feels that needs to be reinforced. "But you are my aunt and Eve is my mother. She's the one who raised me. It can't be any other way."

Karen sets her glass on the table with a bang so loud and sharp it makes Julie jump in her seat. "You have no idea what I've done for you, what I have sacrificed for you."

"I'm sure giving me up as a baby was painful . . ."

"None of this makes sense," Karen says not to Julie but to someone or something unseen. *What's going on with her?* "There is no logic in this."

"Of course it's logical. There is more to being a parent than biology." The moment she says that Julie regrets it. Offended, Karen stands and tells her sternly to "please leave" and climbs the stairs to her bedroom and slams the door shut.

****

Greg paces back and forth in the mansion's Grand Hall, tie loosened and blazer off. He was supposed to go into the office today, but the call Jack received changed his plans.

Jack's dad is dead. The news shouldn't have been so shocking. The man had been ill for a long time. But it was and Greg spent the morning consoling his lover. The two of them sat in bed, naked, with Greg holding him as Jack cried.

Greg is surprised by Jack's response. Father and son spent most of their time avoiding each other or fighting each other. The way Jack always spoke of his old man, Greg expected something else, something other than tears.

After Jack calmed down, they dressed and went upstairs to Joe's apartment to pack. Neither of them said very much, simply because there wasn't much to say. Greg drove him to pick up Little Jack who learned on the way to the airport that the grandfather he never met has gone to heaven.

Ever since hearing the news, Greg can't help but think about his own father. Their relationship was very different. Greg can't remember them ever fighting or talking about anything important. There were no father-son outings or afternoons playing catch. The two shared almost nothing until the end, when Lewis starting reaching out to him.

Greg is determined never to let this happen with his own son. This is why he canceled everything. This is why he's at home. When Johnny wakes from his nap, Greg plans to spend the afternoon with him.

"Dude, that carpet's way too expensive to be wearing it out so fast."

Greg looks over to see Patrick, standing at the Grand Vestibule's threshold, a gentle smile on his face. "I heard you cancelled today. What's wrong?"

"Your timing couldn't be better. We need to talk." Greg motions to the study where his cousin follows him inside. Closing the door firmly, he turns to Patrick. "I know Dad was a member of the Brothers of Thebes." This is a lie; Greg is still not sure if the society really exists. But it seems worth taking a shot --- Especially if he and his own son can follow in a family tradition. "I'm guessing you are, too."

Patrick's eyes widened in surprise, "how the fuck ---" then realizes "shit, you tricked me into that."

"Sorry, but I needed to know."

"That's okay; I'd already decided to tell you."

"So this Thebes group, it's real."

"Yeah, and I'm told the only reason you weren't initiated is because Aunt Lilly didn't want it. But I think she was wrong and so do a lot of other brothers. In fact, there may be a way for you to still become one."

For the next hour, Patrick lays out the plan Alex Mundy described this morning --- without mentioning Mundy's name --- that will allow his cousin to join the Brothers. When he finishes, Greg nods and says simple "let's do it."

****

Ann still hasn't heard from her husband.

She kept the cell on all night, but nothing: no call, no voicemail, not even a text message. The silence is painful and scary. More than once Ann nearly phoned him. But each time she stops herself; if Richard is serious about saving their marriage he'll call.

In the meantime, some decisions need to be made. A baby is on the way. Ann can't keep staying in Julie's old bedroom. And she can't keep the problem a secret; people in towns like Faraway Hill love to gossip. It's a more popular pastime than any game or sport. So she drives the short distance from the Kings to the Gale Farm. A quick knock and her mother answers the door, thrilled to see her. More than thrilled, she's actually beaming because she and Vivian are going over the final details of their very public wedding. The dining room table is covered with books, magazines and notes. Vivian is on her cell taking care of some little problem but stops long enough to wave hello.

Ann notices something. Written on a couple of the notes is the name Vivian Gale. "Is Vivian taking Munroe's name?"

"No, Ann," Lorene corrects her. "She's taking my name. It was her decision. We will both be Mrs. Gale." Ann isn't sure how she feels about that. But it doesn't matter now. Once Vivian ends her call the three women sit down so that Ann can explain the situation. "I'm sure he'll come around," her mother says with all the conviction of a woman who always assumes the best will happen. But Ann has to shake her head and say, "maybe, but I can't count on it."

****

"You can count on me, Mr. Tolliver." Eve and her newest client step out of Shakeen's and into the stifling heat of a Manchester afternoon. "This investment program we've developed is very solid, very conservative."

The client, a professional just hitting 40, nods in agreement. He's getting married soon so he's been making estate plans. "Do you think I will need a pre-nup?"

The question surprises her. It's rare for anyone to raise this issue. Of course, his fiancé is just 22 years old. A leggy, blonde, 22 year old with what Eve is sure must be cheap implants. "That's a very private decision. I suggest you confer with your attorney."

Mr. Tolliver nods again and thanks her for the luncheon. As he walks away down one end of Elm Street, Eve takes the opposite route back toward her office. A block away and her cell rings. Eve glances at the screen to see her sister's name. *This is the last thing I need.* "Hello, Karen."

"You turned her against me."

"What are you talking about?"

"My little girl, my one and only daughter; you tuned her against me!"

"No, I didn't"

"If you had let me tell Julie the truth we'd be a real family now. But you ruined that."

"No."

"Momma always said you were jealous of me and how the boys looked at me and especially how close Daddy and I were." Karen sounds more than angry, she sounds a little unhinged. It reminds Eve of the frightening moment when her baby sister threatened Mark Bradley. She's sure Karen has done some awful things in the past and Eve is worried what she may do again.

"You're wrong, you've always been wrong, Karen."

"We'll see about that."

****

Nick meets them at the airport. Even before saying anything, he gives his big brother a big hug. The act almost makes Jack cry again. Even little Jack joins them in a group embrace. "Hey there little dude," Nick says, inducing his nephew to smile.

During the drive to Briarcliff Manor, Nick briefs his brother on what to expect. "We knew it was coming, we just had no idea when. Mom starting making the funeral arrangements a few weeks ago."

Jack glances to the backseat where his son, properly belted, stares out the window at the moneyed world they are entering. "So, what was it like?"

"I wasn't there when it happened. I was out on a date. Don't look at me like that, dude, Mom insisted. I hadn't done anything fun in forever. Anyway, she called the priest who arrived just in time. I got there about, I don't know, maybe ten minutes after he passed."

Nick makes the turn on Long Hill Road, driving them past the large, handsome colonial homes toward the cape cod where they grew up. Just before entering the driveway, he has one more piece of important news. "He never changed the will."

"You told me that already."

"Did I? Things have been so crazy. But you should know that Mom and I made sure that Dad never saw the lawyer. We even made sure he never called."

****

He still hasn't called.

Almost a full day has past and still, Richard hasn't reached out to her. She has no idea what to think, what to expect. She's is just grateful to Julie and Eve and especially her mother.

"Will there be anything more, Mrs. Davis?" Frederick asks as he directs the maid down the long hall toward her old suite. There is no other place for her then back at the Halloran home. Rumors are sure to start flying almost immediately. Ann can picture people gathering around the famous statute to gossip. It won't stop with Faraway Hill, either.

"There are still a few things in Concord, but they can wait."

Frederick nods and follows the maids. Ann is about to join them when Agnes emerges from her own suite. "I heard you were coming back."

"Julie said its okay."

"Have you heard from your husband?"

Ann shakes her head. She's beginning to suspect that she never will.

"That's such a shame," the old artist says. "He must have a reason."

"Let's just say being New Hampshire's most scandalous woman has
Its drawbacks."

****

Julie was relieved when her husband announced reservations for dinner,
explaining simply that "we both need the break." So instead of a fancy meal in
the mansion's fancy dining room, they drive into Manchester where Greg
surprises her again by bringing her to Piccola Italia.

The two of them used to come here often before their engagement and the
whirlwind life became soon after. They are greeted at the door by the
husband-and-wife team --- Giovanni and Josephine --- who own and run the
restaurant. Giovanni personally escorts them to a private corner, next to one of
the fresco-like scenes of Italy on the wall. "I can't believe you did this," Julie
tells Greg with a warm smile.

"I thought it would be good for both of us."

Giovanni leaves them with some menus. As Julie looks over hers, he asks how
things went with Karen today.

"Not well; she was hurt and angry. Maybe I did it wrong. I told her I love her. I
told her she'll always be my aunt. It's like . . . it's like she had trouble wrapping
her brain around it."

"Maybe you just need to give her time."

"I suppose," she answers, noticing an odd look on his face as if he hopes the
menu would distract him from something but it's not working. "What's wrong?"

Greg shrugs, which Julie interprets as something involving the one person who
has always been between them. "If it's about Jack, it's okay to tell me if you
want." *After all, I may as well get used to having that man in my life.*

"He got a call this morning; his dad died."

"That's a shame, especially after losing Joe."

"They weren't close . . . but I guess we both know what it's like a father. They've
flown down for the funeral."

Giovanni returns to take their order and he recommends a California red wine
called Primitivo, explaining that it will go well with both dinners. Greg has
ordered the Ravioli Stefano but Julie is treating herself to the Chicken Lorenzo.
Actually, it's more like comfort food. Julie has news for her husband, news he

doesn't want to hear. So once Giovanni departs she comes right out and tells him that Ann is moving back into the mansion.

"When the hell is this happening?"

"Right now; she'll be there when we get home."

"The woman just got married. She has a baby on the way. And she's already left her husband. What the hell did she do wrong this time?"

"I don't think that you're in a position to criticize anyone else's marriage."

With that he drops the subject and they start talking about the weather.

****

Double locked doors, a burglar alarm and security lights all deter the common criminal. They are much more reliable than a guard dog or a gun. Any genuine security expert will confirm this. So it's no surprise that Karen St. John has protected her home in this way. It works, too, for most intruders. But an Enforcer is no ordinary man and with his training, Alex Mundy easily enters the house.

Even though it's early evening, the summer sun is still shining. Alex is able to explore the rooms without needing to flip a switch or use a flashlight. Karen has turned this old house into a stunning showplace. Except, of course, for the living room which he notes is strangely devoid of furniture.

Upstairs, he finds the file box in Karen's closet. It's just as Patrick described it. The contents are disturbing. *I can't believe this is the same girl.* The young woman Alex knew was sexy and vibrant and fun. She didn't have --- or at least, didn't seem to have --- a cruel bone in her body. *How did she become like this? Or is this the real her, the real her I never knew?*

He returns it to the shelf to be retrieved later.

Through the closed window comes the sound of a car pulling into the driveway. Karen is home. Alex arranged for some distractions so that he could get in discreetly. This, too, is part of an Enforcer's training.

Alex can hear the front door open and close; of Karen climbing the stairs. He moves to a corner of the bedroom. Surprise is another important skill for an Enforcer.

Karen stops at the threshold. She can sense someone is here, so Alex doesn't bother to hide anymore. "Hello, Karen," he says through the semi-darkness.

She jumps at the unexpected voice. "Who's there?"

"It's just me."

Karen flips on the ceiling light. "Oh my God . . ."

She still amazing. Her figure hasn't changed much since the days when she wore a pale blue maid's uniform. Alex steps up to her and smiles. "It's been a very long time."

Karen stares at him, as if she can't believe it's the same man she knew all those years ago. "You've . . . you've gone a little gray."

"And you are still beautiful."

She closes her eyes and takes a deep breath as if trying to prove that this moment isn't a dream. When she opens them again, Karen surprises him: with a hard slap to his face, a slap so surprising and so strong it makes his cheek sting and eyes water.

"I guess I deserve that."

"You deserve to die. You abandoned us; you wanted me to have an abortion!"

"My father wanted the abortion, not me."

"Where have you been? I've spent years looking for you."

"I dropped off the face of the Earth."

Alex can see the confusion and frustration in her face. Karen clearly wants to do something to him, hurt him in some terrible way, but she can't think of anything. "You should pay for what you did."

"I have paid. I was a conceited, arrogant, entitled young man who bowed to whatever her father ordered. And then I lost everything: the money, the family . . . you and our little girl."

"She's turned against me," tears start to trickle down Karen's face. "After all I have done for her, for us, she left me just like you did."

Alex takes her in his arms for the warm embrace of former lovers. "She'll come back to you, someday. Just as I have."

"I want to kill you," Karen answers, her damp face pressed against his chest. "I planned to kill you."

"Now, why would you want to kill the man who loves you, the man who gave you such a remarkable daughter?" Alex then adds something he knows will have an effect, "where is the logic in that? Didn't you daddy teach you to see things from all angles?"

"Yes, of course."

"This is the start of a brand new life for you, for everyone."

"It is?"

"Yes, my love. But you need to relax." Alex guides her to the bed where she lays back, head against the pillow sham, as she looks longingly at him. The prince has come for his princess. "Now, close your eyes and rest."

Karen does as she is told, and is so happy that she barely feels the needle pierce her skin.

EPISODE TEN

Denise Sullivan forces herself out of bed. She has never been a morning person, preferring to spend long night's club hopping to find the right party or the right guy. She stumbles to the bathroom, relieves herself and looks in the mirror. More than one hook-up has told Denise that she looks sexy with bed head. But seeing her reflection this morning makes her doubt their honesty. Maybe it's because she is now walking up with the thought, *what the fuck am I going to do?*

A year ago she was single and free and having the time of her life in Manhattan. Now Denise finds herself working for a scary, wealthy widow with too many secrets. Even Faraway Hill is losing its charm; the town these days is swarming with tourists.

Showered and dressed, she descends the stairs to emerge in the warm summer air. Already the town square is buzzing with people checking out the little shops or taking cell phone pictures of the John Halloran statue. She grumbles a bit at the corner coffee shop while waiting for her daily latte standing behind of group of old women from Albany debating what to order. Once she is sufficiently caffeinated, Denise begins the short walk to Mrs. St. John's house wondering with each step what bizarre thing to expect next.

A moving van sits on the street. Eduardo is standing beside it with a couple of burly men. He's trying to flirt with one of them who is clearly not interested while his buddy looks on with amusement.

"Good morning," Denise greets the decorator with false cheer. "You came earlier than we expected."

"Well, I knew Mrs. J. wanted her new living room furniture as soon as possible, so here we are!"

The three men follow Denise inside where she expects her employer to be sitting in the dining room with her newspaper and her usual breakfast. But no one is there. *Oh, great, what shit is happening today?* She leaves Eduardo with the movers as they start bringing items from the van. The kitchen is empty and so is the study. Mrs. St. John is not anywhere on the wrap-around porch. Denise goes upstairs where she sees the door to the master bedroom is ajar. The sight sends a shiver down her spine as if some intuition inside her is issuing a warning.

Denise cautiously pushes the door open to see her boss' inert body sprawled across the designer bedspread.

****

Jack Campbell is sprawled across the bed, clad only in his boxer-briefs and staring at nothing in particular.

Spending the night in his childhood bedroom was an odd mixture of the familiar and the strange. The furniture is a faux early American style. The wallpaper pattern is a series of sailboats floating against a blue background. Some of these ships are covered with posters of sports heroes who are now past their glory days. Sitting on the shelves are dusty old copies of *Beowulf* and *Huckleberry Finn* along with football, baseball and soccer trophies. Stuck in the edges of the dresser mirror are snapshots of pals from school and summer camp. One is from college, of him and Greg Halloran laughing at something. Another is of Jackie Westbrook, looking sexy in a bikini standing on a beach.

Aging copies of *Playboy* and *Hustler* are hidden under old briefs in a dresser drawer. In the closet are long forgotten clothes, including a pair of well-worn jeans.

Jack recognizes all of these things, but they seem to belong to someone else who happens to be named Jack Campbell.

A couple of quick knocks and he turns his head to see Nick, wearing a robe, standing at the open door. "You awake, dude?" Jack nods and motions him to come in. He does so, closing the door behind him. They used to meet here early in the morning, the big brother advising the little brother or the little brother razzing the big brother.

"Is Jack up yet?"

"Shit, man, he's been up a good hour. So has Mom. They're downstairs in the family room."

Jack smiles. Their mother has often talked about grandchildren, and his son seems to have taken to her. Of course, she has been giving the boy most of her attention.

"You know she's going to bring it up again, Jack." At dinner last night she asked him to come back permanently and take over the family business. But he said then what he says to Nick now: "I can't do that to Little Jack. He needs some stability. The last thing he needs right now is another big change in his life. Besides, Phil Baxter has been eyeing the managing director's job. Let him have it; I'll chair the board and come in for meetings."

Nick nods and both brothers find themselves in an awkward silence until the little brother says, "I don't think I'll miss him."

"I don't know," Jack answers ruefully, "you were always his favorite. Besides, we <u>will</u> miss him. I even cried after you called."

"But you hated him more than anyone."

"No, dude, I never hated him; not really. But I do wish like hell he loved me, or at least loved me more than he did. He sure as fuck never approved of me. But when it comes to my own son, I'm never going to make that mistake."

****

"Mom, I thought we were going to have breakfast together."

Ann has just arrived at the Gale Farm. The temperature is rising and it is sure to be a scorcher. But Lorene insists on showing her something first. She leads her daughter to the barn. The place was a rattrap during her childhood. Ann always hated going in there, dealing with the animals and the smell of manure. It was repaired and repainted last year and now looks like something from a stylish magazine. They stop at a door tucked away toward the barn's rear. Ann isn't quite sure if she's even seen it before. Lorene slips a key in the lock and opens it.

The room is a memorial to Munroe Gale's life. There are photos all along the walls from Ann's birthdays, school events and family trips. A battered old metal file cabinet has the faded drawings of a little girl to her daddy; all hung with promotional magnets from feed suppliers and hardware stores. A layer of dust clings to every surface.

"This was your father's private place; he came here when he wanted to be alone."

"You mean Munroe came here to drink alone."

"Look around you."

Ann frowns, wondering what the point is. She turns to see a photo tacked to the wall. It's one of seven-year-old Ann standing next to Munroe while attending one of Applecrest Farms' fall weekend festivals. Both are smiling. She remembers that trip to Hampton Falls. It was one of those extended periods during her childhood when he was sober. Lorene steps next to her, takes Ann's hand and says softly, "He died here, in that chair."

Seeing the battered old chair behind the battered old desk hits her in the gut. She is starting to understand a few things, things that her mother tried to explain on Ann's last visit: Munroe wasn't a bad man, he wasn't always a bad father and he loved them. She has too long demonized him in her heart and her memory.

But before she can say anything, mother and daughter are startled by a sudden, high-pitched noise piercing the air.

****

The siren can be heard from one end of Faraway Hill to the other. People open their doors to see what's going on. Shopkeepers and their customers look out plate glass windows. Tourists turn their gaze from the statute of John Halloran. Everyone's attention is drawn to the ambulance as it enters town and rushes past the square where it comes to a stop at an elegant old house with a wrap-around porch.

****

A sedan none of the neighbors recognize comes to a stop in the driveway at Four Corners. A handsome, middle age African-American woman emerges and strides confidently to the door where she tells the housekeeper "I'm Mrs. Bickel and I need to see the senator." When the housekeeper hesitates, her guest becomes so insistent she nearly pushes her way in.

Vivian finds Richard sitting alone in the living room. He is wearing jeans and an open collar shirt. She has never seen him so casual before, or so depressed. The man hasn't shaved in days and his eyes have dark circles. He stares at the glass in his hand, the glass that holds just a finger of bourbon.

"It seems to me," she says as a greeting, "that our last conversation didn't have much impact."

Richard looks up, surprised to see her or anyone. "I've really fucked things up." Vivian sits across him as he hands her a piece of paper. It begins with the words "Dear Richard" and goes on to explain how Ann loves him "more than you can know" and how "my past mistakes have hurt you" but making it clear that she won't stay with a drunk. Setting it aside, Vivian says to him, "can you blame her for leaving?"

He shakes his head and takes a sip of bourbon. "No, but she's right about being New Hampshire's most scandalous woman. Whether she means to be or not, that's what she is. I live a very public life. Her scandals are my scandals."

Vivian takes the glass from his hand; it's not doing him any good. "I thought you preferred scotch."

"We're out."

"It doesn't matter; you've had too much."

"Does Ann know that you're here?"

"No and neither does Lorene; this is my idea."

"Then give me your speech and be gone."

"No speech, but a question."

"Fine; out with it."

"This has to end somehow and at sometime; how do you want that ending to be?"

"I don't know."

"Then I suggest you figure it out right away."

****

For all the things that frighten Eve King about her baby sister, she is starting to realize that the scariest of all may be losing her.

She and Julie are in the waiting room of Elliott Hospital. Neither of them are patient waiters; both women are pacing albeit in different directions. Only Denise Sullivan is sitting. At least, she's barely sitting: the girl is wearing a skirt that to Eve looks like it's painted on.

Like everyone else in Faraway Hill, mother and daughter could hear the ambulance and its wailing siren. Eve was in her kitchen savoring a morning coffee. Julie had just finished breakfast and was conferring with Frederick, the butler. Eve got the call. In a panicked voice, Denise Sullivan explained what she saw. Without even phoning ahead, Eve got into her car and stopped at the mansion. The trio then raced into Manchester only to be stopped by the frustration of the torturous waiting room.

Eve knows that Julie is blaming herself. She can see it in her face. Eve's own first reaction is that Karen attempted suicide but both Denise and a paramedic explained that is unlikely: there were no pills, no gun and no note. Something else happened; something else that will leave Eve alone in the world. Her father is gone as is her mother. Ben is lost to her. Despite everything, Karen remains her only link to Eve's younger self. This frightens her.

"Maybe you should call Greg," she suggest to Julie who shakes her head. "He'll want to rush right over and there really isn't anything he can do here. Besides, I need to know more first."

Dr. Jane Singh, the emergency room doctor, finally appears. She looks tired, as if all of her energy has been expended quickly. They met her briefly over an hour ago in the mad rush of crisis. Eve is the first to ask: "what is it?"

"Your sister had a stroke, Mrs. King. There was pressure on her brain caused by some fluid. We don't know why or how it formed, but we are dissolving it slowly to minimize any additional damage."

"Additional damage?"

"It's too early to be certain, but at this point I only see a partial recovery. You will likely want to look into some kind of long-term care facility."

****

Greg Halloran is sitting nervously behind his desk, fingers drumming the blotter and watching as Patrick explains the plan to their cousin. But the famous Quiet Halloran remains quiet, revealing nothing in his poker face. Robert could be an impediment, although Greg isn't sure why he'd want to be.

They are in the Halloran offices at the Millyard. Both Greg and Patrick have meetings today, so they insisted Robert meet them here.

Once Patrick finishes, the Quiet Halloran turns to Greg and says, stone faced, "are you sure you know what your getting into?"

"I'm a Halloran and so is my son. Being a Brother is part of the Halloran legacy. We should be part of it just as you guys are."

"Do you understand what that entails?"

"If you're talking about the sexual aspect, I'm cool with that."

"Are you cool with keeping it a secret from your wife --- or your boyfriend?"

"My mother knew."

"Lilly found out by accident. Julie and what's-his-name can never know. What the fuck good is it having a secret society that's not a secret?"

"Fine; I'll never tell Julie or Jack. So, is this a go?"

Robert finally betrays a little emotion, something that Greg reads as something close to family pride. "I think I can convince the Elders."

The intercom buzzes. "I'm sorry for interrupting, Mr. Halloran," his secretary, Mrs. Stone, apologizes, "but your wife is on the phone and she says it's urgent."

****

News travels fast in small towns. By late afternoon everyone in Faraway Hill knows about what happened to Karen St. John. Or, at least, think they know. The one certain fact is that she was rushed into Manchester by ambulance. That leaves the townsfolk to theorize and gossip.

At the dollar store, owner Mitch tells his customers that Karen suffered a heart attack. At least, that's what he's heard. A few doors away at the barber shop, Carl says that someone broke into the house. Mrs. Johnson at the corner market is sure its food poisoning. Over at Hugh's Bar, Hugh and his regulars talk about little else. Everyone has his take.

One of the last people to hear the news is Peter Brandt. He has spent the day up in Concord, in a conference with other law enforcement officials from around the state. It was helpful, informative and often boring. Peter knows something is up when he enters the Faraway Hill station and every suddenly falls silent and try not to stare at him. Darlene, an old school friend and a recent addition to the force, motions him aside. She breaks the news to him.

"When did this go down?"

"This morning, but no one has heard anything more. I'm really sorry, Peter. I know she means a lot to you."

****

There are decisions to be made. Hard decisions: the kind of decisions that Julie has never expected she would ever make. Unfortunately, Karen has left her no other choice. An hour ago, her lawyer faxed over copies of Karen's living will and will. Both name Julie. But what disturbs her most is how Karen refers to her: as Julie Mundy Halloran.

"She must have been deep in Karenland," Eve said on reading the name.

Julie, her mom and Greg are sitting in the mansion's oval blue room, surrounded by wallpaper and upholstery in similar shades of the same comfortable color. Dr. Singh has warned them that "the next 24 hours are crucial" and to be prepared to place Karen in a long-term facility.

"Why not the same place as Aunt Katherine?" Greg suggests. Patrick's mother has been living in a home in Concord called Harris Hill Center since she had her own stroke almost three years ago. "I haven't visited her in a long time, but Patrick says the treat her well and she likes it there."

"I like that idea," Eve nods in agreement. "Especially since Concord is so close. We can visit her on a regular basis."

Julie also nods; it seems like a good choice but she wants to visit the place first. Despite everything Dr. Singh has told them, she still feels guilty. Greg reads this in her eyes and says "it's not your fault."

"You can't know that."

"Julie, you heard the doctor: it was fluid on the brain. It would have happened no matter what." Seeing the earnestness in Greg's face just proves once more that Agnes is right. He will make a better friend and a husband.

The mood is broken when Ann waltzes in and declares "well, Richard has agreed to meet with me tomorrow morning."

Julie frowns, Eve rolls her eyes and Greg looks like he's ready to punch her. Ann is aware of Karen's heath crisis --- nothing else --- but acts oblivious to it. Or, at least, that it pales compared to her little marital spat. "We are all glad to hear that," Eve answers receiving a smile and a wave from Ann as she waltzes back out the door.

****

Jack experiences the same strange dissonance of his bedroom in every part of the house.

The Campbells' home was constructed by his grandfather, part of a process to bring legitimacy to a family that initially built its fortune as Manhattan slumlords. It's an attractive cape cod, somewhat out of place among the colonials and Georgians that dot Briarcliff Manor. He knows every corner, has a memory connected with every room and yet the house seems almost alien.

Wandering into the living room, Jack finds his mother sitting peacefully on the sofa. There is even a little smile on her face. She still looks very much like the old pictures Jack has seen of her, as debutant Elizabeth Burton, the pretty girl who charmed society and an arrogant yet handsome John Campbell.

"Hey, Mom, how are you holding up?"

"I'm fine." On Jack's last visit, at Thanksgiving, the two of them didn't get a chance to speak. His father was too busy yelling obscenities at him. His mother was too busy weeping.

"Where's Little Jack?"

"He went for a walk with your brother. They'll be back by dinner. Thank you, by the way."

"For what?"

"For making me a grandmother. When I found out . . . well, when I learned about the other boys I didn't think it would ever happen."

"I like girls, too Mom."

She nods. "Yes, I know. And Nick has explained about Jackie."

"You okay with all this?"

"I couldn't be happier."

****

Arranging everything makes Ann feel a little like a theater director. The setting is the Halloran garden. The time is early morning, while the temperature is still comfortable. A painted wrought iron table with matching chairs is placed on the stone walkway. She even made a quick trip last night to the Mall of New Hampshire and found just the right outfit: a simple but pleasant canary yellow summer dress. All that's missing is her leading man --- who arrives on cue, escorted by Frederick. Husband and wife kiss and hug in a natural, affectionate manner that surprises even them. Once the butler leaves to fetch breakfast, they sit at the table where awkwardness returns.

Richard breaks the silence with a simple, "I'm very sorry." Ann can see in his eyes that he's sincere --- and sober. "Your right, I was letting other people get to me; especially that prick Mark Bradley."

"What other people?" she asks just before the answer comes to her: "Oh, I see, your aides --- and I'm guessing your daughter --- were coming down on you for marrying New Hampshire's most scandalous woman."

Richard nods, embarrassed, like a little boy who let his pals tell him to stay away from a girl they dislike. "I kept brushing them off until I came face-to-face with him."

Their conversation takes a pause as Frederick returns with coffee and orange juice and to tell them that their omelets will be ready shortly. Once he's gone, Ann picks things up where they left off by asking "what exactly happened with Mark?"

He describes arriving to meet with Bradley at some tacky highway motel where the escort greets him wearing nothing but a cocky smile and a pair of tight, white boxer briefs. "I thought I should dress up for this, dude." The whole thing was over in twenty minutes. The man signed the papers and got his money. "Give my best to the Mrs." were Mark's last words.

It's just as Ann expected. "Which means you began having second thoughts about us when we learned I was pregnant; and that news left you feeling trapped."

"Yes, and I'm ashamed of it. You were the victim and I was blaming you for making me a victim, too."

"Where does this leave us?"

Richard explains that he wants their marriage to work, but wasn't lying when he said that he'll be tied up in Washington. "The governor named Linda Powers to hold the seat until November; she doesn't plan to run for it, though."

"I guess this means Adam Newman will be our next senator."

"Probably, but the party does want me to help recruit someone. But even if Newman wins, I know him and I'm sure I can work with him."

Still, she's cautious. "How do we save our marriage if you're putting in all these long hours?"

"I've been thinking about that," he answers and lays out a proposal: that she stays at the Halloran mansion during the pregnancy, where there is a full staff to help. He will fly in every weekend for them to spend time together. "This way, we can spend the next few months rebuilding things between us."

Ann nods, pretending to like the plan even it sounds to her like something his chief of staff came up with. Certainly, using the staff and her pregnancy as the reason she's moved back to Faraway Hill while Richard serves the people should play well in the media. And it salves his guilt. So, she agrees with a smile.

Now, she has one more thing to deal with. She now has to deal with Peter.

✳✳✳✳

It could be worse. That's the consensus of the staff at Elliott Hospital. Dr. Singh explains that while Karen will survive, a full recovery is a long-shot. Greg holds Julie's hand throughout; he insisted on coming with her and Eve.

After the briefing they visit Karen in the ICU. She is lying quiet, eyes clothes and wearing an oxygen mask. An IV tube and various wires are connected to her body. Her hair is a little mussed but still retains the basic shape of her expensive coiffure. Karen St. John has the look of the world's most glamorous patient.

The visit doesn't take long. As they walk quietly and somberly toward the exit, the three are surprised by the appearance of Peter Brandt. He is carrying some flowers and a sad expression. "I'm really sorry about your sister, Mrs. King."

"Thank you, Peter. I heard that things didn't end well for you two."

He shrugs. "That doesn't matter anymore. How is she?"

"Not good; she's going to live --- thank God --- but some decisions have to be made."

✳✳✳✳

Denise is sitting in her boss' refurnished living room. She thinks these pieces are not quite as nice as the first set, but the space looks wonderful. Too bad her own prospects aren't so rosy.

Yesterday morning's stresses left her exhausted. But she still needed to come back here and make sure Eduardo and his men finished. Denise relishes the quiet. She considers taking a nap when her cell rings. It's Julie Halloran calling to tell her that she and Mrs. King are visiting a nursing home in Concord later today. "I guess that means Mrs. J isn't getting better."

"It's not that bad; she'll live and probably recover somewhat. But she won't be able to live on her own anymore."

Denise agrees with a request to stay in the house for the time being, but in ending the call she can't help wondering *what about me?*

✳✳✳✳

What about me is the question Ann asks herself all morning. She barely has her husband and she has lost Peter. She is living with a family that still will not call her own of their own. And there is a baby to consider. *What about me* consumes her, even in the mansion's informal family dining room. Here she sits quietly with a curious Agnes Gabler, pushing pieces of chicken around her plate and thinking about the question over and over.

"You keep that up and I'm sure the chicken will start fighting back."

"What?" Ann looks up, startled. "What did you say?"

"You seem very distracted. Is it about Karen? I know that everyone is worried."

It takes Ann a moment to remember that Agnes is talking about Karen St. John's stroke. She hasn't thought much about it. "No, it's something else."

Agnes is about to ask for more when Frederick appears to announce her daughter's sudden arrival. "Hello, Scarlet, dear; why are you here?"

"I have great news Mom: the house is finally ready. You'll be able to go home soon."

****

Home for many people is the Harris Hill Center in downtown Concord. This is a handsome, red brick building with curved driveway and graceful portico. Even though his aunt has lived here for some three years, Greg Halloran has never visited her. He barely remembers Uncle David's wife just as he barely remembers Uncle David. But Patrick comes often to visit his mother. So he joins the administrator in guiding Greg, Julie and Eve through the facility.

The first thing Greg thinks is that the place is much nicer than he expected. While not opulent, many of the common areas remind him of a better-quality hotel. The dining room is especially elegant, with its subtle wallpaper and teal window treatments. Several residents and their families are in the rear garden, enjoying the flowers and gazebo on a warm summer afternoon.

Every resident's room is personalized. Each comes with standard furniture --- simple, but attractive oak beds, dressers and nightstands --- but other than the medical equipment mounted to the wall it could almost be anyone's bedroom. Long-term residents bring photos, memorabilia and even bedspreads from their homes.

Greg, holding her hand throughout the tour, can feel Julie relax. She is under enormous stress. He is impressed with her resiliency but even her natural strength has its limits.

They arrive at Aunt Katherine's room. She is sitting up in her bed, reading. To Greg's eye she looks a little older than she should --- Katherine is roughly Eve's age, but has streaks of grey in her hair and a few more creases in her cheeks ---

but otherwise is the same graceful woman he saw on brief visits from school. "Hey, Mom," Patrick says after he kisses her. "You look a lot better today."

"They adjusted the dose. I had been on this new medication and I was having the most awful response to it. But I'm much better now. And is that Greg? Why, I haven't seen you since you went of to New York."

Greg smiles. "Hello Aunt Katherine. This is my wife Julie, and I think you remember Eve."

"How could I possibly forget Eve Scott; I was so sorry to hear about your husband."

"Thank you, Katherine. I appreciate that."

"And now your sister, too; well, I know as well as anyone how these things can happen. But the people here have been wonderful to me. Patrick can tell you that when I first came to Harris Hill I couldn't say a word or barely move. But look at me now. I may have to spend the rest of my life here, but at least I can live it. There are all sorts of social activities and we go on outings to downtown all the time."

Soon they all take seats around her bed to hear Katherine Anders Halloran describe a pleasant life of attendants, physical therapy, guests and activities. Greg can see that not only is Julie feeling better about Harris Hill, but Eve is as well.

This could be the right answer after all.

✳✳✳✳

Some of the older folks in Faraway Hill still refer to the Halloran mansion as The Big House. Even today, as Peter Brandt makes his rounds through town he hears it in the gossip. Some of it is whispered, much of it is not. Peter has learned over the years to ignore such things. But this afternoon he overhears one of the Halloran maids at the bakery tell two local grey hairs --- Mrs. Stimson and Mrs. Berman --- the latest: "the farm girl, Ann Gale --- or whatever she calls herself now --- she's back. She's moved completely back in. We on the staff thought for sure it was temporary, especially since the senator had breakfast with her this morning. But nope, it looks like she's there to stay."

The possibility that Ann's short marriage may be over percolates in the back of his head for the next few hours. The only thing that keeps it from going too far is his constant reminder that Ann is pregnant. Still, when his shift is over Peter is compelled to walk up to The Big House and ask to see Mrs. Davis.

Frederick, the butler, escorts him through the ornate Grand Vestibule through the stunning Grand Hall and into the oval Blue Room. The wait is brief, as Ann cautiously enters with a confused look on her face. "You wanted to see me? Is something wrong, something with my mother?"

Peter shakes his head. "No, it's about you . . . and maybe about us."

Ann visibly steels herself in place, waiting for what is sure to be a blow. "First, Ann, I'm sorry I was so cruel the other night. But you hurt me and besides, I was telling you the truth about my parents."

"Okay."

"It's all over town that you've moved back in here."

She rolls her eyes and even chuckles a little. "That figures; what would Faraway Hill be without its gossip?"

"Does this mean you and Richard has broken up?"

"I don't know; not officially, not with the baby on the way. But I think we have for all practical purposes."

"I'm very sorry."

"Thanks; so is telling me that New Hampshire's most scandalous woman is causing scandal all you came here for?"

"No," he steps up to her, takes her in his arms and kisses her deeply, passionately, to the point that her knees buckle.

✲✲✲✲

Vivian wants nothing more than to take Lorene into her arms for a passionate kiss. Being together again after all these years apart makes Vivian feel young. She'd love to do something romantic and sexy and spontaneous. The best Vivian can do in a small town like Faraway Hill is suggest they go out for dinner. But when she finds Lorene, her lover is sitting on a rocker in the front porch staring off into space.

"Lorene, sweetheart, what's wrong?"

"Oh, just thinking about things."

"Don't worry about Annie; she and Robert love each other. Give them time and they'll work things out."

"I hope so, but that's not the only thing I'm thinking about."

Vivian sits in the rocker next to her. Cool breezes make the warm summer evening more comfortable. "What else is there?"

"Karen; we're the same age and her stroke just came out of nowhere."

"Honey, that's the way these things are. You can't do anything about it. None of us can."

Lorene rises, walks over to the railing and looks out at the distant highway. "I know, but I keep remembering what it was like years ago. We were so young, so full of life, making all our friends a little jealous by working in The Big House. Karen and I spent a lot of time together in those days, but I never really got to know her. We share so much, our lives are so connected, yet we're almost strangers to one another."

"Are you wondering about the choices you've made, that she's made?"

"Yes," Lorene responds sadly.

"We can't change the past, if I could change mine I'd have stayed here with you and Annie. But we can't spend our days looking back."

"I know; your right. I just can't seem to help it tonight."

Vivian rises, steps over to her lover and takes Lorene into her arms. The action has nothing to do with passion and everything to do with love.

****

The attendant returns to retrieve her tray. Whenever possible, Katherine prefers to have her meals in the Harris Hill dining room. Its simple elegance reminds her of the refined life she used to lead as Mrs. David Halloran. She also likes being among people, even if they are ill and struggling. The more cognoscente patients often have great jokes or interesting stories to share.

But tonight is different. Tonight she is expecting a visitor, a very important visitor. The visitor has not called ahead. He doesn't have to. Katherine knows that he is coming. The events of the day confirm it. So when his tall, handsome and graceful form appears at her door she doesn't even have to look up from her crossword. All she has to do is say two words.

"Hello, Alex."

EPISODE ELEVEN

Alexander Mundy gently, quietly closes the door behind him. "Good evening, Kitty."

"No one's called me Kitty in years," she chuckles. "Not since I lost my David."

Walking further into the room, Alex notices the photos on the dresser and the walls. They depict a small but loving family: of David and Katherine at their wedding; newborn Patrick; the trio on vacations and their son on the soccer field. Alex always wanted a family like this.

"You've gone a little grey," Katherine says with a sad sigh.

"And you are as beautiful as ever."

"And you are still the best liar I know."

He pulls a chair next to the bed and sits. It has been years since these two old friends have seen each other. "I'm surprised that you were expecting me."

"David and I had no secrets from one another. You know that; he told me all about the Brothers long ago. Of course, I haven't said anything to Patrick. Has he had his final initiation?"

"Yes, and he did very well. He's a full Brother now. It won't be long before Matthew is, too."

"Matthew is sweet; he always sends me something for my birthday and at Christmas. It's a shame Lilly blocked her son from joining."

"We've found a way to change that. Greg will become a plebe through a special program. After that, all of the Halloran men will be Brothers."

"Good; that's the way it should be. I take it you are here about Karen Scott."

"How did you know?"

"I didn't; it was a guess. Her stroke sounded a little too convenient to me. But what I don't know is what she did to deserve it."

Alex hesitates; everything about the situation saddens him. "She killed a Brother and his wife."

"Anyone I know?"

"It was . . . Lewis and Lilly."

"That makes no sense. She was miles away when Lilly died. And didn't that man Gale confess to killing Lewis?"

"Karen has been very good at covering her tracks." He can almost admire her for it.

"Well, she wasn't always so . . . adept, I guess is the word. After David and I were married she tried to seduce him. She tried more than once. Whenever he went to Boston on business Karen made damn sure they ran into each other. Apparently when she left Faraway Hill she began climbing the ladder on her back."

Alex frowns but he doesn't answer. He's seen Karen's files. He knows much of what she did: whom she seduced or blackmailed or killed on the way to becoming Mrs. St John. "They wanted me to eliminate her, but I couldn't do it."

"Of course not; it was asinine of the Elders to ask you. I take it that you want me to keep an eye on her after she moves in."

"Harris Hill does full background checks on everyone they hire. It would be too difficult for us to manufacture a watcher's fictional history in time. Because of the method I used, she'll stabilize quickly."

Katherine's smile has a small trace of wickedness, of a woman looking forward to doing something deliciously naughty. "I'd be happy to help."

****

Julie spends most of dinner just moving food from one side of her plate to the other. She's not in a mood to eat or do anything else. No one seems to be. Greg is barely eating anything; Patrick declined dinner and is in the study, reading. Ann is upstairs as Frederick explains that "Mrs. Davis prefers to dine alone this evening."

That leaves three people sitting around the big table in the Halloran's family dining room.

It isn't just the situation with Karen that bothers her. Julie wasn't expecting Agnes' news. "Scarlet came by today to tell me that my sugar house is finished." Julie pretended to be happy for her, but the truth is she likes having the woman around. Agnes notices this and tries to lighten the mood with one of her colorful tales, this one about George Burns and Jack Benny trying to one-up each other with jokes at a party. Julie and Greg both laugh at the appropriate moments, but the atmosphere doesn't change.

No one bothers with dessert and they all retire early with Julie wondering why some things change and so many other things don't.

****

Tomorrow is the big day. Everyone in Faraway Hill is talking about it because everyone in Faraway Hill has been invited to it. Peter Brandt is surprised. Lorene Gale has always been a shy woman, one who preferred to stay in the shadows. Yet she is turning her wedding into a community celebration.

As he walks to town hall for an early morning meeting with the mayor, he sees workers putting up a stage, Greg Halloran jogging around the square and people staring at everything from a sidewalk.

Faraway Hill's little town hall is a simple, wood frame building that has been standing in the same place for as long as anyone can remember. The clerk and mayor and their few aides work on the first floor. The top floor is for archiving and council meetings. When the whole town needs to convene, they do so in the basement.

Mrs. Oswald greets him with her usual, knowing grin. Harriet Oswald isn't as old as she looks, but the bun and graying hair make her appear to be from an earlier time. As town clerk, she handles nearly every form of paper Faraway Hill issues or receives or processes. She also loves to gossip. "Its so sad what has happened to Karen Scott."

"Yes, ma'am."

"She is so young to have a stroke. I hear they are moving her to a home in Concord."

Peter doesn't want to talk about Karen. The pain and the embarrassment are still a bit raw. "Are you looking forward to the big event?" he asks her. It is well know that Mrs. Oswald has, at best, mixed feelings about same-sex marriage. But she surprises him by saying, "Very much. I've never seen Lorene so happy. She finally found someone who is good to her and she has a grandchild on the way."

The gruff eighty year old mayor appears at his office door. Without a greeting or a preamble, Francis Fitzgerald motions Peter to join him. There are last minute security issues regarding the wedding to discuss and a man with few years left to him isn't interested in wasting any time.

****

Karen is awake. The nurse told Eve that as she arrived at Elliott Hospital this morning. "She's doing better than anyone expected." They've transferred her sister out of ICU and into her own private room. Eve tries to be upbeat when she sees Karen, who is lying motionless in her bed. Only her eyes indicate awareness, widening at Eve's forcibly cheerful "good morning."

Eve is a terrible actress. A tear trickles down Karen's cheek, a sure sign that she understands the situation. Eve sits in a chair next to the bed and reassures her sister that "Julie and I are doing everything possible to help you" and explains this afternoon's move to Concord. "It's a really nice facility. They've got staff there to help you recover so you should expect lots of therapy. Besides, with Katherine there you will have a friend. And Harris is so close to Faraway Hill that we can visit you often."

It isn't helping. Another tear crawls its way down the side of Karen's face. Eve tries a different approach: "I need you to get better. First we lost Daddy and then Mom and then Ben; I can't handle losing you, too."

Karen's eyes look down, as if to say she's feeling sad. At least, that's how Eve chooses to interpret it. "I know that things haven't been good between us, especially lately. There were times when you frightened me. Its true, Karen, there have been moments when I was sure you were capable of some scary things. But that doesn't matter any more. You're my baby sister and you gave me your daughter to be my daughter. And that is a gift I will always cherish."

****

This is the kind of day one should cherish: sun shining, not a cloud in the sky, weather warm and humidity mild. Julie doesn't bother with the car. Instead she decides to walk from the mansion to Karen's house. It should do her a world of good.

A sweaty Greg meets her at the end of the long, curved driveway. He's started jogging around the square again. "Good morning," he greets her. "You were still asleep when I got up." The two of them have had separate bedrooms for months.

"So much has happened; I needed the rest. By the way, the hospital called. Karen is doing incredibly well. They will let us move her to Harris Hill this afternoon."

"That's fast; I would think they'd want to keep her for awhile longer."

"Me too, but Dr. Singh says the sooner she's in treatment the better. Can I count on you to help?"

"Of course," he smiles. "Patrick and I already planned on it, not matter when the move happens."

Julie can't help herself and leans over to give his damp cheek a kiss. "Go shower, you stink" she teases him. Greg winks at her and continues up to the mansion.

Strolling through Faraway Hill Julie starts noticing a familiar face among the townsfolk and tourists. It takes her a moment to realize that it's a governor --- not New Hampshire's governor --- but one that she has seen periodically on the news. Seeing him reminds Julie that the quadrennial "circus" is about to begin: would-be presidential candidates visiting the state with the country's first primary. *No matter what happens,* she thinks, *life really does go on.*

Julie spends the rest of the morning with Denise. The two women pick out items that Karen will need or want while in the nursing home. Julie reassures her aunt's assistant that she'll be taken care of; Julie and Eve have already decided to give Denise six months' severance to help her finance a return to New York.

****

Wealth can be seen at every corner in every town throughout Westchester County. This is where New York City's old money elite --- families with names like Rockefeller, Astor and Vanderbilt --- have lived for generations. The little village called Tuckahoe is no different. As small as it is, each building reflects privilege and permanence. This is especially true of the stately Catholic parish. These stones have been burnished by sun, wind, rain and snow for over 150 years. Many important people have been married here, christened here and mourned here. The latest of these is financier John Campbell.

Jack is surprised to see so many people. His father was neither popular nor beloved. Yet, every seat in every pew is taken. Attending are business associates, distant cousins and representatives of the different Catholic charities John Campbell supported. The biggest surprise for Jack is the appearance of Eddie Grant and his wife, Judy. He and Eddie were occasional fuck buddies at college and Jack had hooked up with Judy once shortly before she met Eddie. The couple acts to the entire world like a contented twosome. But Jack knows the only reason they married is because Eddie got Judy pregnant. *I wonder why they came to the funeral.*

The service seems unbearably long to him, with the various prayers and hymns finally culminating with the rite of commendation. Little Jack fidgets from time to time, but mostly behaves himself. The boy has certainly taken to his new grandmother. They've been nearly inseparable the entire visit.

After the pallbearers --- the old man specifically prohibited his sons from being among them --- take the casket out to the adjacent cemetery where John Campbell is put into the ground.

The guests then gather in the parish's vast, ornate Community Hall where one-by-one each person offers his condolences to Elizabeth and her two grown boys. When Eddie and Judy take their turn, Eddie greets Jack with a wink. The last time the men saw each other was just after Thanksgiving. Jack needed Eddie to check some documents and Eddie charged him a blowjob for the service. They haven't spoken since. "It's nice of you to come," Jack says to them. "But I didn't realize you guys even knew my dad."

"Dude, didn't he tell you? I got a job with your father's firm last month. Now that Phil Baxter is moving up to managing director, I'll be his right-hand man."

****

Julie likes the room. Harris Hill has assigned Karen a large space with a window overlooking the pretty garden and its charming gazebo. Greg and Patrick have volunteered to help her. Together, the trio hangs some of Karen's favorite pictures, cover the bed with her pricey duvet and do everything they can think of to create the elegant environment Karen St. John has grown accustom. Julie wanted to bring some of her furniture as well, but Harris Hill insists on using their own.

By late afternoon, Karen is brought in on a gurney. Denise and Eve accompany her, carrying some personal belongings. The medics carefully transfer the patient to her new bed. "Karen," Eve says trying to sound cheerful. "Haven't Julie and the boys done a good job with the room? The photos are especially nice. I didn't even know that you had a framed copy of Daddy and Mom's wedding portrait."

Karen remains silent. Only her eyes are active. They seem to reveal a myriad of things, from fear to frustration and even a touch of anger. Everyone pretends to ignore it and act as if Harris Hill is something close to a resort. The group leaves by dinner time, each member promising to visit her soon, knowing that only a few will keep their promise.

****

Every blank canvas is a promise waiting to be fulfilled. That's the way Agnes Gabler has always approached a new work. She is sitting in her suite at the Halloran mansion, putting the final touches on her most recent painting, the mansion's exterior, created in her signature primitive style and splash of color. She will give it to Greg and Julie as gratitude for being her host these last several months.

Agnes has mixed feelings about leaving. She misses her sugar house, the place she grew up and spent nearly all her life and where she finds unlimited inspiration. But it can be lonely, isolating, to be far away from people. Here she is able to vicariously enjoy the ups and downs of being young.

Frederick, the butler, enters after a polite knock on the door. "Are you fished with dinner, madam?"

"Yes, thank you. It was delicious."

She wonders why he's cleaning up and not one of the maids. She also wonders something else: "Did I hear Robert Halloran a little while ago?"

"Very possibly; he has returned to Los Angeles."

"I also thought I heard Joan."

"Mrs. Lansing, her son and husband, arrived late this afternoon. I believe they were invited to tomorrow's wedding. They are dining with Mr. and Mrs. Halloran at the moment."

Agnes is surprised that Lorene would invite Joan Halloran to her wedding. But, then, there is still much history that she doesn't know. "I wasn't aware that Lorene and Joan were that close."

"I suspect Mrs. Gale invited all the Hallorans as a courtesy to her daughter."

"That was nice of her."

"Indeed." Frederick places the last dirty dish on the tray and looks around to see if he's missed anything.

"Frederick, weren't you here when Karen and Lorene were on staff?"

"Yes, madam; they were hired by my predecessor."

"You must have known them quite well."

Frederick arches an eyebrow; he knows he's being drilled. "No, madam, I did not." With that, he picks up the tray and takes it, with whatever he knows, out the door.

✶✶✶✶

Ann has finished her dinner. She is in her own suite at the far end of the mansion. These were Joan's rooms growing up. It still has the fading rose wallpaper Greg's aunt hung as a teenager. It suited the faux French Provencal furniture that Ann replaced with nicer things the first time she moved in.

She spent much of the morning trying to figure out what to do. Her marriage is all but over in name. Yet, to see Peter in any open fashion will surely create more scandal. Ann doesn't need that any more than do the two men in her life.

Then an idea came to her.

First, Ann drove to a computer store not far from the Merrimack called PC Authority. The helpful staff helped her pick out everything she needs without asking any pesky questions. She then drove to the other end of Manchester, to nondescript warehouse near Massabesic Lake. Ann paid a premium to have the Mr. Messenger delivery service take some of the equipment to the Brandt home right away.

Shortly before dinner, Ann installs the software on her laptop, connects the camera and tests the microphone. Everything works; she just needs to wait.

And that's precisely what she's been doing for hours: waiting.

Finally Ann hears the signal she's been waiting for. She sits in front of her laptop and sees on the screening the handsome, smiling face of Peter Brandt.

"Isn't Skype, cool?" Ann giggles.

****

Jack was hoping that Greg would be picking them up at the airport. Instead, Denise appears with an apology. "They moved Mrs. J into the nursing home this afternoon. He's been helping Julie."

"I'm surprised they moved her so fast."

"Me, too; but the doctor says she's stable enough. Besides, the sooner she gets treatment the more likely she'll recover."

The drive back to the apartment is short. But all the activity of the last few days has left Little Jack exhausted; it doesn't take much for his father to put him to bed early. He and Denise spend some time catching each other up assisted by a generous supply of red wine. "I'm glad the old man didn't disinherit you," she tells him.

"The thanks should go to Nick and my mom. They're the ones who kept the lawyer at bay. Say, did you learn anything more about Karen's weirdness?"

Denise shakes her head. "I don't think we're ever going to know more. Julie has already promised me a big severance so I can go back to New York. Personally, I don't see how the woman is going to recover."

****

Mark Bradley likes having William Jackson as a client.

The man has just turned forty, yet regular sessions with a personal trainer keep him lean, and defined. He is extremely wealthy being the owner of property in all five boroughs of the city. William and his pretty wife regularly appear in the society columns. Their three children attend the finest private school in Manhattan. William is a man with power, influence and stature. He also indulges a detailed and imaginative fetish with an open wallet. And that's what Mark likes best.

William has created a very special, very private playroom in the basement of one of his many buildings. The space has faux marble floors and walls and pillars. There is a pond with a fountain, colorfully erotic frescoes and sofas to lounge upon. In this fantasy world the impressive and imposing William Jackson plays the role he enjoys more than husband, father or tycoon. In that world he is a Roman slave, obedient to his master, Marcus.

Mark loves this game. William wears a tunic and Mark a toga. Mark gets to call him "bitch boy" and make him do humiliating things. Tonight's session involved William feeding his master with his hands, massaging his master's sore muscles and even holding his master's cock as he pisses into the pond. The evening culminated the way it always does: Mark fucking him doggy-style on the floor as the multimillion cries out, "whatever pleases my master!"

William pays triple Mark's normal fee for these sessions.

Once back home, Mark first washes away the sweat of Ancient Rome in a hot shower. He then plops naked on the leather sofa and turns on the TV. He has earned enough for the next several days. It's time to relax.

Flipping channels, he speeds through repeats of "Friends" and "Frasier"; an old black & white Humphrey Bogart movie; some sort of infomercial about a knife that can slice concrete. None of it looks interesting until he lands on CNBC. Over the anchor's shoulder is a photo of the crazy bitch who nearly ruined his life. "It was confirmed today by a spokesperson for the St. John Group that Karen St. John, widow of late financier Martin St. John, has suffered a stroke in her Faraway Hill, New Hampshire home . . ."

Mark roars with laughter; *she deserves it* he tells himself.

****

Matthew Newberry pulls the blanket over his head. It doesn't work: the sun's light is too strong. Besides, he can hear the shower. Matthew gives up and throws the blanket to the floor and cautiously opens his eyes. The first things he sees are the smiling faces of Uncle David and Aunt Katherine. It takes him a moment to get oriented and remember where he is and what he is looking at.

He spent the night in Patrick's suite --- formerly Greg's rooms --- because the other suites are full. Matthew slept on the parlor sofa. The smiling faces come from the wedding portrait of Patrick's parents.

Most of Greg's personal belongings have been moved out. This is Patrick's domain now. His track trophies sit on a table, photos of girls and guys from college are stuck in the dresser mirror; and yesterday's clothes are in a heap on the floor. Only the furniture remains unchanged. It is still the heavy, masculine mahogany that Greg grew up with and that Patrick is keeping.

"It's about time you woke up, dude."

Matthew turns to see his cousin standing a few feet away. Patrick's hair has been properly gelled and he's wearing a towel around his waist. Matthew didn't even hear the shower stop. "Yes, sorry."

"No problem."

Someone knocks on the door. Patrick calls to let them in. Greg enters and immediately asks Matthew with a wry smile, "es vos meus frater?" The young man is taken aback by hearing his cousin speak the formal Brothers greeting. Patrick chuckles and explains about Greg becoming a plebe. "I'm sure I'll need your help," Greg says to both of them.

"You bet," Matthew grins.

✳✳✳✳

"You have to be there," Ann insists. She is trying to stay calm but the hand holding her cell is trembling a little. *If he bails on me today I'm going to be really pissed.* Richard, on the other end, pleads that "I'm expected in Washington."

Ann is sitting in her suite, at the far end of the mansion, in her slip getting ready for the big day. At least she's trying to: her stomach has felt queasy since she awoke.

"No, you're expected in Faraway Hill. It's my mother's wedding! Damn it

Richard, how do you think it'll look? The *Union Leader* and the *Monitor* will be there, not to mention Channel 9. I can just imagine the headlines: 'Senator Skips Mother-In-Law's Same-Sex Wedding.' Is that what you want?"

She can hear him sigh in frustration. Ann knew that invoking the threat of bad publicity would get to him. "Okay, I'll pick you up as we planned. But I can't stay all day. I have to fly to Washington."

"Just make an appearance with me, that's all I ask." Richard promises that he will and they end the call without saying another word. *I guess this is what my marriage will be like from now on.*

Ann's stomach begins to churn again. *Is this morning sickness? Fuck, I don't need that today.* She sits for a moment to relax and allow things to settle. It seems to work. Someone knocks on the suite's door. Ann puts on her robe and announces "come in."

Frederick enters, caring the dress she is wearing today. Ann picked it out at a little boutique in Concord a couple of weeks ago. But as she's begun to gain weight, it needed some altering. Fortunately, the downstairs maid is a seamstress. "Good morning, Mrs. Davis."

"Good morning, Frederick." A small amount of turbulence returns to her tummy. "Is Mrs. Halloran awake?" *Maybe Julie will have some advice about how to deal with morning sickness.*

"Mrs. Halloran left early this morning on a special errand. She should be back in time for the wedding."

****

Jack lets his son sleep. Attending another funeral so soon after his papa's as worn the boy out. Clad in boxer briefs and an open robe, he quietly brews a cup of coffee and turns on the TV (making sure the sound is low) to catch-up with CNN. He considers calling Greg when someone knocks on the door. *Maybe that's him.* Tying the sash, he walks over and opens it and sees not Greg Halloran, but Julie Halloran standing in the hall.

"I hope I didn't wake you," she says with the business-like demeanor of someone on a mission but trying not to be rude about it. Her appearance disorients him. Julie is the last person he expects to ever visit him. "Ah . . . no, I've been up for some time. Jack is still asleep."

"Then we can make this brief. May I come in?"

Jack steps aside to allow her to pass. Trying to think of something to say, he tells her that "I'm sorry about your dad. I really liked Ben. I wish my own father was more like him."

Julie glances around the apartment. "Growing up all of my friends said the same thing."

"And I really appreciate how . . . tolerant you've been about me and Greg, and especially about losing Joe."

"There has been enough tragedy. You just lost your own father, too. Then there is Aunt Karen . . . well, I guess I should get to the reason I'm here."

"Okay."

"You and I are not likely to ever be friends, not true friends. But we are going to be in each other's life for a long, long time. For Greg's sake and for our sons, I'm willing to call a truce."

"Really?"

"No more arguing or pettiness. We will be civil to each other when we meet. And you will respect that Greg and I have a connection and a son."

"Of course."

Her mission accomplished, Julie declines his offer of coffee. But, at the door just before leaving she tells him something more. "Go to the wedding. I'm sure Greg will like to see you. Besides, the whole town is coming out. A couple of more people won't make much difference. Just don't embarrass me. These folks don't know what I've been through."

Jack is surprised at the invitation. "Are you sure you want Little Jack and me there?"

"We have to start somewhere. Besides, in many ways, it's an historic event."

✴✴✴✴

In the year John Halloran and his firm completed the main buildings in Faraway Hill, it didn't make news. It didn't even create a ripple. There were more important things going on in the world. His own mills in Faraway Hill and Manchester hummed along creating magnificent cloth. At the same time, that other Manchester --- the first Manchester --- was rocked by an historic event: spinners went on strike demanding higher wages.

It was also the year the Emperor Napoleon annulled his marriage to the famous Josephine so he could marry an Austrian duchess. Only months later another Frenchman, Nicolas Appert, would invent a new method of preservation that would change forever the way people store and consume their food.

Thousands of miles away, Spain began losing its American colonies. Argentine started the dominoes falling when it declared independence. Even further away a warrior-politician named Kamehameha unified a collection of Pacific islands to create his Hawaiian Kingdom.

People were quietly born, people whose lives would make plenty of noise, including composer Fredric Chopin and the ultimate showman P.T. Barnum.

It was also the year the Chevalier d'Eon died. He served France admirably as a diplomat, soldier and even a spy at the Russian court. He also spent his last thirty years living as a woman --- complete with a brand new wardrobe bought with royal money.

But this day, this time, its two women who bring focus to the little town built by the textile baron. There have been other same-sex marriages in New Hampshire. But none are like this one. When Julie Halloran called it "historic" she didn't mean it with irony. When Vivian Bickel suggested to her fiancé that they "invite everybody" she didn't mean it as a metaphor. Literally, everyone in town is welcome.

The ceremony itself is held in the Faraway Hill Unitarian Church. It was originally built as an Episcopal church a century ago and it still has many of its original elements like beamed ceilings, carved woodwork and stain glass windows. The sanctuary is too small for everyone, so cameras and large video screens in the town square allow everyone to participate. Seated in the crowded church are Ann and Richard, who try to act like the loving couple. Peter Brandt isn't far away; he and Ann glance at each other but are careful not to say or do anything.

Greg Halloran and his wife Julie sit together. Next to them are Julie's mother, Eve King and the famed artist Agnes Gabler along with her daughter Scarlet and grandson Bobby. In the row behind them are the Hallorans: Joan, Patrick and Matthew along with Joan's young husband. Paul Lansing spends much of his time gaping at the church and the people inside it.

The moment has arrived: Lorene and Vivian appear together wearing similar, but not identical dresses. They stroll down the aisle as a couple and stop before Pastor Elizabeth. The matronly woman is clad in a simple robe and sporting a broad smile. "It is always God pleasing when two people --- any two people --- come together in love and respect and joy."

It's a short ceremony. The two women exchange simple vows, rings and a kiss. Pastor Elizabeth ends the rite with the words, "I am pleased to present Mrs. Lorene Gale and Mrs. Vivian Gale."

Outside, around the square and the famous statue of John Halloran, the entire population of Faraway Hill has gathered. Streamers, balloons, a stage, food tents and other items create the feel of a community festival. People cheer and applaud and throw rice at the couple as they emerge from the cozy church.

Ann Davis was right about the press coverage: not only are the *Union Leader*, the *Monitor* and WMUR here with reporters and photographers, so are TV stations from Boston. There has never been so public a wedding celebration in New England, much less one that marries two women.

People eat and laugh. Others dance to the swing band. Kids make crafts and grown-ups sample boutique beer. Greg and Julie Halloran hold hands and smile happily as they walk through the crowd. When they encounter Jack Campbell and his son, Julie prevents the moment from being awkward by shaking Jack's hand and giving the boy a hug.

The other Hallorans mingle with the townsfolk, with Patrick and Matthew amused as Joan plays the role of elegant matriarch.

Senator Richard Davis and his young wife make the rounds, greeting constituents and accepting congratulations on the baby. By late afternoon the senator has gone, leaving Ann to discretely make plans with Peter for that evening.

Eve King encounters friends she sees every day and those she hasn't seen in months. Each of them expresses his sadness over Ben and Karen. Eve accepts these condolences graciously.

Fans gather around Agnes Gabler, who has set up her own special spot in the square to regale them with her colorful stories.

Denise Sullivan quietly slips out of town.

Off in the distance, watching discretely, unnoticed by everyone, Alexander Mundy watches his daughter with her family. And he smiles.

****

Katherine Halloran smiles as she watches coverage of the big day in Faraway Hill. "In an unusual act of community," explains the reporter, "the newly married couple has invited the entire town to celebrate with them. From what I can see, it looks like everyone in Faraway Hill accepted the offer. When I spoke to the two Mrs. Gales --- and yes, they are using the same name --- the ladies said it was because the townspeople have been supportive and accepting of their relationship from the very beginning."

As the reporter continues with her coverage, the visuals switch to clips of the crowd. Katherine is especially pleased to see her son among them. *David,* she thinks, *would be so proud.*

A knock and one of the nurses, a charming Hispanic woman named Rosalie and Katherine's favorite on the staff, comes in as scheduled. "Are you ready?"

"Absolutely." Rosalie helps her move from the bed to the wheelchair, which the nurse pushes the short distance to another room. It's a large space with a window overlooking the pretty garden and its charming gazebo. Lying in the bed, unable to move anything but her eyes, is Karen Scott St. John.

Rosalie leaves them alone to "get reacquainted". Once she's gone, Katherine wheels herself closer to the bed. "Hello Karen, remember me? I'm Kitty Halloran." Karen just stares at her. "You've done some pretty bad things. Attempting to seduce my husband; killing my in-laws and trying to murder my nephew. All that time I was helpless to do anything; I didn't even know what was going on. But how things have changed. I'm going to have a lot of fun with you here."

Karen's eyes speak louder than any words she could utter. They scream fear.

Book Three Discussion Guide

This guide has been created to facilitate book clubs and their members in discussing *Faraway Hill: Book Three.*

- *Faraway Hill: Book Two* ended with a cliffhanger leaving the reader to wonder who had died in the King's Korner fire. Did you have a theory as to the victim? Were you right?

- Karen's mental state becomes more unbalanced. She even tears apart her living room in a rage. Yet, Denise stays in her employ despite her growing fears. Would you have done the same thing? If not, would you have quit or made a third choice?

- Julie is shocked to learn of her adoption and especially that Karen is her mother. Have you ever known someone who discovered as an adult that they were adopted? How did they handle the revelation? How do you think you would have?

- Greg becomes Julie's single biggest supporter and she acknowledges that. Have you ever known estranged spouses who come to each other's aid in a crisis --- or have you known them to move further apart? What does this say about Greg and Julie? Is Agnes right, that they are better as friends or should they have tried to save their marriage?

- Was Richard right to second-guess his marriage to Ann? Why or why not?

- Sudden death is a big part of *Faraway Hill: Part Three* as a trio of funerals changes the lives of the characters. How has death affected your life?

- Mark stays in town for Ben's funeral, but the author doesn't delve into his feelings about it. How do you think Mark felt about losing his father?

- Should Ann forgive Munroe, the only father she knew growing up? Why or why not?

- Jack tells his brother that he never hated their dad, but wished their dad had loved him more. Have you known complicated parent-child relationships? Which do you think is more challenging, father-son or mother-daughter?

- Ann finds first comfort, then rejection and comfort again with Peter. As the trilogy ends it is clear that they plan to continue their secret affair. Would you if you were them?

- Have you ever had to put a loved one in a long-term care facility? If so, how did it affect the family?

- Normally the Brothers of Thebes would execute someone who hurt one of their own. But for sentimental reasons Alexander Mundy and his fellow Enforcers refuse to kill Karen. So a compromise is reached. Do you think they made the right decision? Why or why not?

- Considering their history with commitment, do you think that Greg and Jack can truly have a successful, long-term relationship?
- The trilogy ends with an unusual town celebration: the wedding of Lorene and Vivian. Have you ever attended a same-sex wedding? How do you feel about same-sex marriage or civil unions?
- Would you like the author to continue the *Faraway Hill* sage in additional novels?

www.ingramcontent.com/pod-product-compliance
Lightning Source LLC
Chambersburg PA
CBHW070957120726

47910CB00004B/1273